Mail Order Brides Collection:
Jessie's Bride
Montana's Bride
Caleb's Bride
Marshall's Bride
Husband of the Bride

By Susette Williams

Family Friendly Fiction

Published by Family Friendly Fiction
© 2017 by Susette Williams

Scripture taken from the HOLY BIBLE, NEW INTERNATIONAL VERSION®. Copyright 1973, 1978, 1984 Biblica. Used by permission of Zondervan. All rights reserved.

The History of House Springs, Missouri

While this story is fictional, House Springs is an actual town. In the late 1700s, a man named Adam House settled on property that has a large spring. The area became known as House's Spring, and eventually became known as House Springs. I can only imagine what the area was like in the 1800s, which is when this story takes place. I remember how I thought it was the 'boonies' when I first moved out to the area in 1983. It has grown quite a lot in the last thirty+ years. When I first moved out here, we didn't have fast food restaurants. There were only small diners. My husband and I opened our own bakery, which we operated for a little over 18 years. I miss the bakery…or the baked goodies…and I also miss hanging out with the locals. It seems life has become more complicated and busier, even though we've got all the new-fangled inventions to help make our lives easier. I'm not sure it's working…

Mail Order Brides: Jessie's Bride

By Susette Williams

CHAPTER ONE

House Springs, Missouri — 1843

Jessie Kincaid stared at the captivating picture of Sarah Engle, his future wife. While the drawing was done with pencil, she'd told him her eyes were blue and her hair was blonde. He envisioned gently tugging on one of the curling tendrils piled up on her head and it bouncing back into place. He smiled, laid her picture aside and began to write.

My Dearest Sarah,

Your picture along with your letters, and getting to know you, has only served to capture my heart. I know that we can build a wonderful life together. I have enclosed a ticket for the stagecoach, along with ten dollars so that you have some money for your journey. I look forward to seeing you soon. I am anxious to start our new life together and cannot wait to finally see you face to face.

All my love,

Jessie

He folded the letter and placed it, along with the stagecoach ticket, inside the envelope.

Being the youngest of four had its drawbacks, especially since he didn't have any sisters for his brothers to fuss over. It meant his brothers' overbearing, protective side was focused on him, whether or not he wanted to deal with their interference in his life.

Jessie never knew the one sister their parents had the year before he was born. She'd caught pneumonia and died before Ma became with child with him. If she had lived, his brothers would have focused on her and not Jessie. But since they didn't have a sister, they focused on him, the baby of the family.

Out west, there were twice as many men folk as women. Perhaps even a few less in their town. Long hours tending cattle didn't give much chance to cultivate a proper relationship with a woman, much less with competition for the few handsome women there were in town.

None of his brothers were married, even though his oldest brother was twenty-eight, a mere four years older. How would they handle him getting hitched before they did? Moreover, how would Ma handle it, especially since she hadn't even met her future daughter-in-law? He would have told them he was writing a mail order bride except he didn't want to endure the ribbing his brothers would have given him.

Sarah would be there in a couple of weeks. That didn't give him long to break the news and let it simmer in before they had a chance to meet her. Hopefully by then, his brothers would be on their best behavior. He could hope.

Jessie folded the envelope and stuffed it in his pocket before heading to the kitchen for vittles.

"Smells good, Ma." He gave her a brief sideways hug and brushed a kiss upon her cheek, then snitched a piece of bacon off the plate.

"Don't think I didn't see that, youngin'." Ma smiled and brushed a few stray hairs away from her face with the back of her hand. She always wore her hair in a bun, ready for work.

Jessie winked at Ma and took a bite. "The whole point of cookin' is to eat it."

"Well, let her finish cookin' so we all can eat." Marshall sounded gruff, but Jessie knew his brother had a tendency to show his dominance. Which was needed to keep the peace in his job as sheriff. Being the oldest Kincaid boy, keeping his three younger brothers in line, had prepared him for the role.

Out of all his kin, Jessie feared telling Marshall about his fiancée more than anyone else. Marshall figured most people had an angle, and he'd want to check Sarah out before he'd give his approval.

Jessie turned twenty-four last month, he wasn't getting any younger. Pa was only forty-two when he died eleven years ago. If Jessie wanted a family, and wanted to have time to enjoy them, he needed to get started. Maybe it was better to wait and tell his family until Sarah was here, then they couldn't do anything. Marshall would understand the law, and the legal ramifications of breaking an engagement. Not that Sarah would take him to court for a broken love pledge, but her pa might. Marshall'd have to allow Jessie to go through with the marriage.

"What are you grinning about?" Caleb asked as he and Montana came in from outside and both took a seat at the table.

Jessie hadn't realized he was smiling. If he wasn't careful, he'd end up giving himself away.

Marshall got up and grabbed the plate of biscuits and bacon from Ma and set them on the table. "He's grinning 'because he got away with snitching vittles before everyone else." Marshall playfully slapped the back of Jessie's head. "Take your hat off and say grace."

Jessie obliged, placing his hat on the back post of his chair. He smiled as he said the prayer over their meal, silently adding special thanks for his bride-to-be.

CHAPTER TWO

Sarah Engle stirred the soup in the cast iron pot over the fire outside their wood shack. Pa would be back from town shortly with her brothers, Elijah and Zeke. They were picking up supplies. She had wanted to go as well, so she could get the mail before Pa. He read most of her mail if he got to it first. Of all the suitors he'd made her write, she only cared about receiving a letter from one of them—Jessie Kincaid.

Taggie, their stray black and white bulldog, perked up, his tongue hanging to the side as he began to pant. Sarah looked up and saw dust rising in the distance as a wagon neared their shack. It was Pa and the boys. While it had been dry lately, the dust flying indicated they were in a hurry. That couldn't be good. Sarah stood and wiped her hands on her apron that covered her faded pink, floral dress. Her heart raced quicker than a stampede of wild horses.

Pa pulled the wagon to a halt and hopped down, not bothering to wipe the dust from his well-worn trousers. He'd apparently gotten another small tear in them she'd have to mend after supper. Sarah noticed his clenched fist. He had an envelope in one of them that he flung at her. "You wanna tell me the meaning of this?"

She bent to pick it up, not taking her eyes off of Pa the whole time. He must be fuming 'cause neither of her brothers dared get down from the wagon. Before she could even pull the paper out of the envelope with trembling fingers, Pa grabbed a handful of her hair in his fist. She winced in pain.

Taggie hunched down on his front paws and barked at Pa.

"I told you not to go gettin' sweet on any of them fellas." Pa shoved her with the fistful of hair he had.

Sarah fell to the ground, still clutching the letter.

"You know I had no intentions of letting you marry that fella, or any fella, unless they had money and could provide for me and your brothers as well."

"I'm sorry, Pa." Her voice quivered.

"We been on this here property a little over four years now. It's almost ours." Pa ran a hand through his hair as he paced back and forth in short strides. "I promised your brothers that we'd stay put unless something better comes along and now, because of you, we may have to leave."

"Jessie's family has a ranch," Sarah tried to sound hopeful. If Pa would just go and check things out, he'd see that Jessie had potential. She knew he did—he had to.

"You can forget whatever foolish thoughts you have about that youngin'," Pa said. "He's the youngest of four and ain't likely to inherit much of anything."

"You want us to start packing up, Pa?" Zeke glared at Sarah but didn't verbally vent his frustration. The look he gave her, along with his clenched fists and stance spoke volumes

Elijah brushed a stray tear off his cheek with the back of his hand and stood in silence next to his brother. They knew it didn't do any good to argue with Pa. Once he made his mind up to do something, he did it, no second guessing.

"Here's what you do." Pa stopped pacing, turned and glared at Sarah. "You write that boy back and you tell him your aunt has taken ill and that you had to use the stagecoach ticket to go see her instead. Tell him you are sorry you can't even think about marriage right now."

"But I don't have an aunt," Sarah protested.

"Don't act like you ain't lied to fellas before." Pa spat on the ground. "You weren't supposed to give this boy your real name, but ya did, and if you don't make this right, I'm gonna have to go against my promise to yer brothers. Would you rather have them hurt instead?"

Sarah shook her head. She didn't want to hurt Zeke or Elijah, nor did she want to hurt Jessie. But would Pa really make her marry someone else just because they would take care of them as well as her? Didn't it matter how she felt? It mattered to her, and whether or not Pa liked it, she was seventeen and old enough to choose whomever she wanted to marry. She shoved the letter from Jessie into her pocket and extended her other hand toward Pa. "Give me the stagecoach ticket and I'll exchange it tomorrow when I send the letter back to Jessie."

She'd write the letter to make Pa happy, but she had no plans on sending it to Jessie. Sarah took a deep breath and slowly exhaled as a plan played out in her head. "I gotta work at the restaurant tomorrow night, so I'm gonna spend the night with Maybel."

Pa nodded. He was always agreeable when something meant making money.

Now at least Sarah would have a reason for taking a change of clothing with her when she left tomorrow, and she'd have a reason for not coming back tomorrow night.

By the time Pa figured out what she was doing it would be too late for him to do anything about it.

CHAPTER THREE

Jessie rubbed his eyes and blinked a couple times, sure it would clear the image in front of him. It didn't work. The woman standing outside the general store, shielding her eyes from the early afternoon sun while she looked around was young, beautiful, and had curly blonde hair piled up on her head. He'd been dreaming about those curls for a couple months. But it couldn't be her. Sarah wasn't due for another week at least.

A grin crept up before he even realized he was smiling. If she was here already, that meant she was just as excited as he was to start their new life together. He wanted to shout and yelp with joy. Rather than getting carried away, it seemed prudent to make sure it was Sarah before he made a fool of himself. Jessie took a deep breath and hurried towards her.

A horse whinnied and snorted, catching Jessie's attention. The wagon's driver had pulled back sharply on the reigns. "Watch where yer goin'!"

"Sorry." Jessie tipped his cowboy hat to the man.

The older man frowned, shook his head, leaned to the side and spit chewing tobacco over the edge of his wagon.

Jessie turned his attention back toward the woman across the road. She must have heard the commotion because she was staring at him now.

He grinned.

Her expression remained unreadable. If it was her, she might not recognize him. The Daguerreotype he'd sent Sarah was a couple years old, and it was of his whole family. He'd told her he'd shaved his beard and mustache off that he had in the picture. Their gazes remained locked as he approached.

Jessie stopped a few feet from her. His breath caught in his throat. Her cheeks were slightly flushed. She blinked rapidly, opening her mouth a fraction before closing it. She apparently didn't know what to say either. Which gave him comfort. "You're even prettier than the drawing you sent me."

Her eyes widened. She covered her heart with her hand. "Jessie?"

He nodded and grinned. "Yes, ma'am."

Remembering his manners, he took off his hat and ran a hand through his hair, hoping he didn't have an indentation from his hat.

"I'd forgotten you had shaved." Her blue eyes held his brown ones captive. "I think you look mighty handsome without facial hair, but charming either way."

"Maybe I better marry you before I take you home to meet my three older brothers." Jessie's cheeks warmed. He hadn't meant to say that out loud, even if he was thinking it. "I'm sorry. I shouldn't have said that. I don't mean to rush you."

Sarah laid a dainty hand on his arm. "It's all right, Jessie."

He loved the way she said his name. Her voice sounded musical. When she smiled, he was happy to see that she had all her teeth, and they didn't appear to be in bad shape either.

"I'm ready and I would be more than happy to marry you today if that would make you happy." Sarah leaned toward him and gently touched his cheek.

"Really?" Marrying her right away would save him from having to explain everything to his family and hoping they'd digest it better than pickled pig's feet. One thing the Kincaids were known for was speaking their mind. Sarah might hightail it out of town if his brothers said what they were thinking—given they had a habit of nitpicking when it came to Jessie. If he took her home as his wife, then it didn't matter what any of them had to say. It'd be too late.

"Are you sure you wouldn't mind?" Jessie stammered, and glanced down the street toward the church, then back at Sarah. "The preacher usually takes lunch at the saloon. He might even be back at the church by now." Jessie turned his hat in circles in his hands. "We could go look."

"I'd like that." She folded her hands in front of her.

"Really?"

The sound of her laugh was delicate. She nodded. "Really."

"Well, all right then." Jessie put his hat back firmly on his head and held out his arm for her to grab on to.

Sarah glanced down. "What about my bag?"

Jessie could have kicked himself. Why didn't he think about her belongings? He lifted the tiny suitcase. "Where's the rest of your luggage?"

Her blue eyes misted. She glanced down. "I'm afraid this is all I have."

"Well, we'll have to fix that soon enough." Jessie held out his arm for her again. "Shall we go see the preacher?"

She looked up at him and nodded like a school girl who'd just been told they were going to get a piece of candy.

Sarah took hold of the crook of his arm, and clasped her other hand on top of it, drawing close to him. "I'd like that."

Jessie smiled to himself when he thought about the plain silver ring he'd bought the day he mailed Sarah the letter with the stagecoach ticket. He'd been carrying it around in his trouser pocket ever since.

CHAPTER FOUR

The church was a quaint one-room building containing wooden pews lined with hymnals. An organ and a wooden stand to hold his Bible were on the platform in the front of the church. The walls on either side of the church were lined with windows where streams of sunlight spilled through.

Since they were having an informal wedding ceremony, Pastor Morgan stood on the floor in front of the platform. His wife Mary, who was very far along with child, agreed to stand in as Sarah's witness. Jessie had asked Sam, who helped out at the general store, to stand in as his.

It would have been nice if they had someone to play the organ, but Sarah was happy to just be getting married to Jessie. She smiled at the handful of wild flowers Jessie had gathered for her while she was taking a few minutes to freshen up after her long journey. Jessie was just as thoughtful in person as he was in his letters. Sarah always knew in her heart that she couldn't pass up the chance to become Mrs. Jessie Kincaid. Which was a dream come true moments later, after Pastor Morgan had Jessie place the plain silver wedding ring on her finger and proudly announced they were now husband and wife.

Jessie shouted in excitement, picked her up and spun her around. Their eyes locked as the whirlwind began to slow and her feet slowly eased to the ground. He kept one arm around her waist and reached to cup her face with his other hand. His thumb stroked her cheek for a moment before his lips came down to claim hers. Sarah melted into his arms, savoring the taste of his mouth on hers as excitement danced inside her at his touch.

"Ahem."

Jessie pulled his head away and looked toward Pastor Morgan before letting his hand drop to his sides. "Sorry, Pastor."

"Congratulations to the both of you." Mary leaned forward, tilting her protruding belly to the side as she hugged Sarah.

"Thank you." Sarah's cheeks still felt warm after the toe tingling kiss Jessie had given her.

Jessie thanked them as well, paid the preacher, and took her hand to lead her from the church. "I think we should get a bite to eat and then maybe go over to Aunt Clara's Inn to spend the night."

"Your aunt has an inn?" Sara didn't remember him talking about an aunt. But over the last two years, she had written numerous gentleman, she was bound to get some information confused.

Jessie patted her hand and laughed. "No, silly. That is the name of the place." He paused for a moment on the walkway and looked at her. "You know, come to think of it, I don't rightly recall ever hearing her talk about her kin, other than a husband who passed away when I was a youngin'."

"So, she isn't an aunt?" Sarah found that peculiar.

"I don't rightly know." Jessie laughed and set off again for their destination.

Sarah smiled and squeezed his arm closer to her as they walked. The Good Lord had smiled down at her today and blessed her with a husband beyond her dreams.

She knew in her heart that she couldn't let him get away. That's why she defied her father and journeyed to Festus.

Today was her wedding day, a time to celebrate. Sarah pushed thoughts of her father and brothers from her mind. She'd find a way to ease into the subject tomorrow, after she'd had more time to win Jessie's heart. Then surely, he would be more understanding and forgive her for her part in the deception. After all, her feelings for him were real.

When they reached Aunt Clara's Inn, Sara continued to hold onto the crook of Jessie's arm and carefully grabbed a handful of material to raise the hem of her dress an inch or two to climb the stairs leading up to the establishment. When she reached the porch, she let go of her dress and smoothed the fabric with her hand.

Jessie set Sarah's suitcase down and knocked on the door.

A few moments later, an elderly woman opened the door and greeted them. "May I help you?"

"We'd like to rent a room for the night, Aunt Clara," Jessie announced.

Her eyebrows rose a fraction as she glanced from Jessie to Sarah, and back again. "I'm afraid I don't know either of you and if you are looking to entertain yourselves..." Aunt Clara's tone was demeaning, "then might I suggest you try the saloon down the street. I pride myself on running a respectful establishment and won't have any of those goings-on under my roof."

Jessie quickly took off his hat and extended his hand for Aunt Clara to shake. "I'm sorry ma'am," he stammered. "You might not recognize me. When I was a boy, your husband, Fred, would have my older brother

Marshall help him out with some chores and Marshall would bring me along."

"Oh, my." Aunt Clara clasped Jessie's hand in both of hers. "You're the sheriff's brother?"

Jessie nodded, flashing a lopsided grin. "Yes, ma'am."

Sarah tensed. She didn't recall Jessie ever mentioning his brother was the sheriff. Pa would never have let her continue to write Jessie if they had known. She swallowed hard. Tomorrow she'd make a point of writing Pa and telling him what she'd done and that he couldn't do nothing about it now. She was married to the sheriff's brother. Pa wanted nothing to do with a law-man.

Sarah forced herself to listen to the conversation at hand. Jessie was telling Aunt Clara how they had just gotten married and wanted to spend the night in town, so they could do some shopping for items for his new bride.

"Please, come into the parlor." Aunt Clara led the way to a sitting area with several chairs, a mix of prints and a solid cream colored one, and a floral settee. "Have a seat."

Jessie led Sarah to the couch and allowed her to sit before residing beside her.

"Goodness, my boy, I can't believe you are married now." Aunt Clara sank into a padded chair that looked like it had been well worn. Probably her favorite chair, by the way her body unwound into shape like a woman who'd just taken off a tight fitted corset.

Sarah couldn't help but smile at the thought.

Aunt Clara's gaze warmed as she smiled back at Sarah. "I can tell you both are happy."

Sarah nodded. "We are."

"Then perhaps it's time I got you both settled in your room." Aunt Clara hoisted herself up out of the chair and winked at Jessie.

Heat rose to Sarah's cheeks.

"Thank you, ma'am." Jessie grabbed the suitcase and stood, turning to help Sarah.

When he winked at Sarah, she felt even warmer and wished she had a fan to wave so that she could cool herself off. Or at least to hide her embarrassment.

At the top of the stairs, Aunt Clara announced, "Your room will be at the far end of the hall so that other guests are sure not to disturb you."

By the time they reached their room, Sarah wished she could have a few moments to herself. All her fantasies about getting married hadn't included what went on behind closed doors. Ma died nine years ago, so Sarah never had the chance to ask her much of anything. The only woman in her life that she might have even been able to ask questions, of a personal nature, was the woman that Sarah had worked with the restaurant. While they were close, they weren't *that* close.

Once they were alone in their room, Sarah stared at the pine, four poster bed in trepidation. Jessie set her suitcase down on the floor and drew her into his arms. The air escaped her lungs. As if sensing she needed to be resuscitated, Jessie's mouth came down on hers. Sarah let go as he breathed new life back into her body.

CHAPTER FIVE

"You either open this door or I'm going to break it down!" a muffled, but loud voice yelled.

Jessie's head shot up. Their second attempt at making love interrupted.

"What's goin'—" Jessie covered Sarah's mouth before she could finish asking her question.

"Sh, it sounds like there are a couple people in the hallway," Jessie said. "I know that voice. Get dressed."

Before Jessie could roll over, the door burst open.

Sarah screamed. She scrambled for the cover and pulled it up quickly to keep from revealing herself, accidentally knocking Jessie out of the bed. He grabbed his hat and covered himself to no avail.

"What in tarnation?" The man with the beard and a deep voice glared at Jessie. "You ought to know better than this. Ma will have a heart attack if word of this gets out."

"Marshall, whatever you think this looks like—it ain't!" Jessie threw an apologetic look at Sarah and turned his attention back to the man.

"Marshall?" Sarah was confused. "Is he one of your brothers?"

Jessie nodded, not taking his eyes off the man in question, who seemed content enough to stand there glaring, with his hands on his hips, paying no mind that his brother was standing there without a stitch of clothing, except the cowboy hat he was holding to shield his unmentionables.

Sarah didn't mean to laugh, but she couldn't help it.

"What are you laughing about?" Marshall asked.

His stern look didn't phase Sarah. He didn't look like the type to hit a woman. Now her pa on the other hand…

Sarah shrugged, clutching the sheet closer to her body. "I think it is kind of peculiar that my husband—"

"Husband?" Marshalls eyes narrowed like a hawk barreling down on its prey. Sarah couldn't tell whether she or Jessie was in more danger from his brother. "So, you aren't engaging in sin?"

"No." Jessie leaned slightly to his left to look past Marshall. "Excuse us, Aunt Clara. I think it might be better to discuss this in private, considering…" Jessie glanced down at his unclothed body.

Sarah wanted to pull the covers over her head. As loud as Marshall was in the hallway, no doubt the rest of the guests were bound to be eavesdropping.

"I'd appreciate you keeping this all quiet, Aunt Clara." Marshall's voice was smooth as honey.

Sarah's gaze snapped back to make sure it was the same person. Sure enough, it was.

The sound of shoes shuffling on the wood floor faded, signaling that Aunt Clara had left. Marshall still didn't close the door. He just stared at Jessie for a couple moments, then he reached up, raised his hat and ran his hand through his hair before putting the hat back on his head. "I hate to say it, but I just now realized you ain't a boy any more. Somehow, when I wasn't lookin', you grew up."

Jessie laughed. "I've been grown up for a while now, Marshall. You all just keep treating me like the baby of the family."

Marshall nodded. "I think you are right." Marshall exhaled a deep breath. "And since you ain't a youngin no more, it's your place to break the news to Ma."

Jessie nodded. "I expected to tomorrow."

Marshall turned and grabbed the door handle to go. He paused. "And Jessie, you can bet Ma ain't gonna be happy."

CHAPTER SIX

"You shouldn't have spoiled me." Sarah sighed. They were headed back to the ranch in Jessie's wagon. "Your ma—"

"Our ma," Jessie corrected her. "She's your ma, too. By marriage." Jessie glanced at Sarah. Her eyes held a hint of sadness. "I thought that would make you happy, seeing you said your ma passed away when you were a youngin', just like my pa did."

Sarah nodded. "It does make me happy, but it also gives me worry lines 'cause your family is going to think I only married you for your money."

Jessie laughed. "Why in the world would they think something like that?"

"Jessie, you bought me a new dress, had that nice woman measure me so she could make me a couple more, along with a riding dress and you even ordered me a new pair of shoes and riding boots." Sarah's eyes widened, her voice wavered. "Jessie, I ain't ever owned that many clothes in all of my life. Here we have been married all of a day and…" A tear trickled down her cheek.

"Whoa." Jessie pulled the horses' reins and brought the wagon to a halt. He took off his riding gloves and gently wiped the tears away. "I'm sorry, sweetheart. I didn't mean to make you cry."

Sarah sniffed. "They're tears of happiness."

She didn't look happy to him.

"It's just, I ain't ever had anyone be so kind to me before." Sarah kissed his cheek and he melted inside. "I knew you were the one from the moment I received your first letter."

"Well, good then," Jessie said, putting his gloves back on. "Now, since that's settled, can we head back home, so you can meet everybody?"

Jessie was concerned about Sarah's shaky smile but knew that once she met Ma and his other two brothers, she would be all right. They'd love her as much as he did. He was certain of it.

They rode for the next half hour in silence. When they were getting close enough to see some of their herd grazing in the field, he nudged Sarah gently. "Those are some of our cattle," Jessie said. "You'll see the house in the distance. I'm sorry you won't have your own kitchen, but we can see about building a home by next year maybe. It won't be much, but we would have some privacy."

Jessie smiled to himself. After the interruption at the inn, he liked the thought of privacy and having his new bride to himself.

"Does all your family live in the same house now?" The bonnet he bought her kept a lot of the sun's glare out of her pretty little face, but she still shielded her eyes at times. Especially now, as she stared in the direction of her new home.

Jessie couldn't remember ever living anywhere else, but here. Their house had gotten bigger with time, to make room for growing boys. Jessie and Sarah would be starting their own family. "Marshall's the only one who doesn't live in the main house anymore. He's got a place of his own not far from here. There is still a lot of work he has to do and said it was easier to live there and work on the house in his free time."

"Ah." Sarah nodded thoughtfully.

As they drew nearer to the house, he heard Sarah take a sharp breath.

"What's wrong?" Jessie glanced at her. She looked pale, like she might faint. "Do you need me to stop?"

"Jessie…" Sarah's eyes misted.

"Whoa." He brought the horses to a halt. "What's wrong? Please tell me."

"My pa's here," as she said those words, it sounded like the very life drained out of her.

"Isn't that good?" Jessie reached over and grabbed her hand. "That means we can break the news to him and my family together."

The sadness had returned to her eyes. "My pa told me to write you and tell you that I was going to see a sick aunt. He doesn't want us to be together."

Jessie tilted his head carefully, to avoid the brim of her bonnet, and brushed his lips against her. "It's all right. He can't keep us apart now." Jessie smiled. "We're married."

She opened her mouth as if she was going to say something, and then closed it. Jessie grinned even bigger. A woman speechless. Who'd have ever thought it? He was just happy that he'd taken all her need for worry away.

Jessie urged the horses on and they swayed along the bumpy road in the wagon. If they could survive Marshall's initial shock yesterday, they could survive anything. Ma was more apt to be hurt that she hadn't gotten to come, not that she was sentimental. Sarah's pa might have preferred to be there as well, or at least meet the man who was marrying his daughter. They may not have started their marriage off right, but it would all work out.

No sooner than Jessie pulled the wagon up, two boys started toward them. Jessie hopped down and helped Sarah climb out of the wagon. "Are these the brothers you wrote me about?"

One was slightly taller than the other. Both had brown hair that needed a trimming. The younger one had more freckles than the bigger boy. Did she say they were teenagers? Maybe almost teens? They were shorter than Jessie, and he wasn't even six feet tall. Jessie was the shortest of his brothers by two to five inches, and they didn't let him forget it. If they weren't *older* they were *bigger*. Marrying Sarah was one situation that them being older or bigger didn't matter because there was nothing any of them could do about it now.

Perhaps her brothers wore sour expressions because they didn't have her at home to cook and look out for them. Jessie felt a tinge of guilt. Maybe some widow would take mercy on her pa.

"We need to talk." The taller one-eyed Jessie suspiciously. He was around the same height as Sarah. He grabbed Sarah's arm and started to pull her aside.

Jessie grabbed her other arm. "Whatever you have to say to my wife, you can say in front of me."

The boy's eyes grew as wide as silver dollars.

"Jessie and I got married, Zeke," Sarah's tone sounded sweet, but he could tell she was trying to be pleasant in what might become an unpleasant situation.

"You're gonna be in a whole heap of trouble worse than you already are when Pa finds out," the other boy said.

Jessie felt Sarah shiver beneath his touch. "She's not going to be in trouble with anybody." Jessie drew her to

~ 30 ~

his side. "She's my wife and there isn't anyone else she needs to concern herself with. Now let's head inside, so we can all meet properly and get to know each other."

The living room, kitchen and table where they ate were all in one wide, open area. Marshall was leaning against the wall. Ma and his other two brothers were seated with a man who Jessie assumed was Sarah's pa. A thin man with graying hair, who looked to be younger than Ma, but older than Marshall, hopped to his feet and headed straight for Sarah.

"Hello, I'm Jessie." Jessie stepped in front of her and extended his hand for the man to shake.

The man ignored the offered hand and tried to sidestep Jessie. "Let me talk to my daughter."

"If you have something to say to my wife, you can say it in front of me." Jessie stood firm. He could almost feel Sarah cowering behind him. He didn't blame her. Her pa had a look of pure hatred.

Her pa gave Jessie the once over and planted a fist on each hip. "Fine. You want me to talk in front of you, we'll talk. I intend to have this so-called marriage annulled so that Sarah can marry one of the other men folk that she's been writing."

"Other?" Jessie felt weak in the knees. Sarah had been writing other men? And her pa wanted her to marry one of them? He turned to Sarah. "Is that why your pa wanted you to stop writing me? Why he wanted you to pretend to be going to stay with a sick aunt?"

A tear trickled down her cheek. She slowly nodded. "I didn't want to write them, but he made me." Sarah sniffed and wiped at the tear. "You were the only one I wanted to write. That's why I used my real name."

Jessie decided it would be best to sort through his own emotions later when he had time to think clearer. He needed to deal with the situation at hand now. One problem at a time. "Whatever the reason, we're married now, and we can work this out."

"The only thing we're going to work out is how quickly we can get this marriage annulled," her pa said.

"There ain't no annulling this marriage," Jessie's tone was sharp. He balled his fists. "This is a real marriage in every sense of the word, and now that my wife and I have been together—we're staying together."

This time, it was her pa's turn to look stunned.

Marshall moved closer, while his other two brothers eyed the situation. No doubt ready to jump in if Jessie needed them. Ma was unusually quiet, apparently still in shock by his news. He'd make it up to her later. His brothers had always hated how he could charm Ma and never get in trouble.

Marshall took a couple steps closer. "And since we are all witnesses that you had Sarah writing with the intent to mislead several men, should you try and run off with her or have the marriage annulled, we will be forced to sue you and your daughter for a broken love pledge," Marshall said. "I'll be sure to discuss the matter with Judge Parkins when he gets back into town, since I am the sheriff."

Sarah's pa glanced at Marshall. He may have been pale before, but he looked even whiter now. "Sheriff?"

Jessie didn't want any bad blood between their families. He was still her pa, after all. If he left angry, he might not let Sarah see her brothers again. He didn't remember all the stuff she'd said about them in her letters, and now he didn't know for sure that everything she had ever told him was true, but she did seem fond of both the boys. She must have been like a ma to them.

"I know this has all been quite a surprise to all of you, and you weren't expecting to have to take care of yourself." This may be the time he allowed his family some say. Jessie would make her family an offer, but it would hinge on input from his own family and how they felt on the matter. "So, if you and the boys are in need of a job and a place to stay, if my family thinks we can use the extra help, you can work as ranch hands and stay in the bunkhouse with the other men."

"Are you saying you wouldn't let us stay up here with my daughter?" her pa asked.

"For now, I think it would be best," Jessie said. "My wife and I need to get better acquainted and I sense you make her feel somewhat distressed."

Jessie didn't care about the raised eyebrow, or dirty smirk Sarah's pa gave him. If they were going to work out their problems and get beyond this mess, the last thing they needed was to have her pa making her feel all out of sorts.

If they were ever to become *as one* like the Bible talked about, she was going to have to get away from her pa. And while a part of Jessie wished it could be totally away, the man was still kin. Jessie couldn't expect her to totally turn her back on her father, for her brothers' sake. Jessie would never turn his back on his family either.

CHAPTER SEVEN

Sarah hated lying in bed next to Jessie with his back turned toward her. It was a might bit different than the night before when he couldn't keep his hands off of her, not that she wanted him to. "Aren't you ever gonna forgive me, Jessie?"

"Forgive you?" his voice sounded incredulous. He rolled over and faced her, propped up on one arm, still avoiding actually touching her as if he couldn't bear to near her again.

Moonlight shone through the window, making it easier to see each other's faces. Too bad they couldn't be making love beneath the glow of the full moon.

"I don't know how I am supposed to trust you again," Jessie's words were somber.

It made Sarah's heart ache.

"Jessie, I don't blame you for not trusting me, but you talked in front of Pa like you wanted to work this out, and I do, too. I love you, Jessie, really love you." She wiped away a tear as it trickled down her cheek. "I didn't want to do what Pa had me do. I'd been writing men since before I was fifteen. Pa made me write every one of them because we needed the money to get by. After Ma died, there were days we didn't get anything to eat, and sometimes, Pa wouldn't come home at night. I had to take care of Zeke and Elijah. There's things you do in life that you just don't go around telling everybody. You live through them and you deal with them."

Sarah turned her head away to keep from giving into the grief that threatened to overwhelm her. What she went through was bad enough, but then to have Jessie turn his back on her was downright unbearable.

"You were the light in my darkness, Jessie." She wiped another tear away as it ran down the side of her face. "No one had ever made me excited to get mail. I didn't care about any money or trinkets men sent. I wanted someone to really care about me, and I thought I found that in you."

Sarah rolled over to her side and cried quietly into her pillow. She had no business feeling sorry for herself. She deserved to suffer for her part in this. She didn't know why she had listened to Pa. *Because she didn't have a choice*, she reminded herself, even though it brought little comfort. Jessie was the last person in the world she would ever want to hurt and yet she had.

"Pa will get his way." Her words were a mere whisper, a realization. "It's better for me to leave so I don't hurt you or your family no more."

A warm hand reached for her and turned her back over so he could see her face. She blinked a couple times to clear her vision from her teary eyes.

"Do you love me?" Jessie's voice was strained. No doubt he was dealing with his own emotions of betrayal.

Guilt riddled her heart. "Yes, Jessie. I love you with all my heart. That's why I'm gonna go in the morning, so I don't cause you and your kin no more problems. Because as long as my pa's around, there will always be trouble."

"I can handle your pa," Jessie whispered. "You on the other hand…" He caressed her face in his hand, gently stroking his thumb across her cheek. "I can't handle the thought of losing."

Jessie claimed her mouth with his in a kiss that held the hope of promise and love, and for another night, the two of them became one.

CHAPTER EIGHT

A month later...

"You're looking mighty perty tonight, Ma." Sarah's pa leaned close to Jessie's ma to see what was in the Dutch oven. "Those pies smell delicious. I can't wait to finish dinner so we can eat them. You did a wonderful job teaching my little girl how to cook better."

Sarah wondered what her pa was up to. He'd sure made a point of showing up at the house a lot this past week or so, and as long as she'd known him, he'd never been sugary sweet like he was being right now. She'd make a point to talk to him before he and the boys headed back to the bunkhouse tonight.

"Zeke and Elijah," Sarah interrupted their lounging on the couch, "would you mind washing the forks and setting the table?"

"I'm tired," Elijah whined. "We have been fixing fence all day."

"Mind your sister." The glare Pa flashed the boys was evidence that his true nature was lying just beneath the surface.

He had an angle, she just didn't know what. Her stomach felt queasy just thinking about it.

Sarah helped Ma, as everyone had started calling her, carry the food to the dinner table. All the men were already seated.

"Here, let me get that." Pa hopped up and pulled out Ma's chair. Sarah never recalled seeing him do that for their mother when she was alive.

"Thank you," Jessie's ma said. While she was polite, she didn't seem the least bit charmed by Pa's smooth talk. "I hope you won't mind sayin' grace for us, Jonah."

Sarah almost laughed. It was the first time she'd heard anyone around these parts call Pa by his given name. By the look on the Kincaid boys' faces, they were surprised their ma knew her pa's name as well. They needn't worry. Sarah had seen enough women swoon when they were in love to know their ma wasn't the least bit interested in Sarah's father. He could tell any whale of a story he wanted, the Kincaid boys' ma wasn't going to get caught up in any line he was feeding her.

Pa stammered through it, but to Sarah's surprise he prayed. Evidence that Pa was definitely up to something. Even the pastor back home said that if Pa ever showed up in church, it would be for his own funeral.

After dinner was done, Pa kept up with whatever escapade he was carrying out by offering to clear the table and help with dishes. While Sarah's brothers were listening to Jessie and his brothers tell stories about when they were growing up, Sarah turned to hear Pa and Jessie's ma talking a few feet behind her.

"I'm sorry I never got around to apologizing for my behavior when we first met a month ago," Pa said. "It was all such a shock for me when Sarah didn't come back home the next day."

"I understand," Ma said.

"It's been hard on me," Pa said. "You know, I think it is much harder for a man being widowed. Especially trying to take care of a daughter and raise her right."

"I wouldn't know," Jessie's ma said. "I raised sons and men folk ain't always been too thrilled taking orders from a woman, but I got by." Ma sounded a bit curt. The sound of dishes being cleaned stopped.

Even Jessie turned to see Ma's hands on her hips, glaring at Pa.

"And if you ask me, I'd say your daughter is the one who has been doing all the raising. I don't much blame her for latching onto my son. He's a good man and she could tell that in his letters. At least she's got enough sense to see that, and if you were any kind of a father you would step aside and let your daughter be happy."

Pa's face was turning red, and not because he was hot physically—he was red-hot mad. The part that concerned her was Pa getting quiet. Some people got madder than a wet hen when they were angry. Pa plotted revenge.

Sarah hopped out of her seat and hurried over to interrupt things before anyone got more out of sorts. Sarah forced a smile to her face. "Pa, do you think I could speak with you outside a moment? I had a couple things I wanted to discuss in private."

Pa nodded and didn't say a word, which sent chills down Sarah's spine for some reason. This new leaf Pa pretended to turn over was merely an act. His true self showed when he couldn't manipulate the setting. He liked having control and thinking he had the upper hand in a situation. One thing Pa hadn't counted on was that Jessie's family wasn't buying the act he was selling.

Once they were outside, and a good enough distance from the house that nobody would overhear their conversation, Sarah turned to her pa and planted both hands on her hips. The sun was going down, but it still shone enough that anyone could see them if they looked out a window or came outside. Sarah folded her arms across her chest so that it wouldn't look like she was angry, even though she was. "Okay, Pa. What's going on?"

Pa spit on the ground. "You saw how that woman treated me after I was sweet on her."

"You?" Sarah blinked rapidly. "Wait a minute. Are you trying to tell me you really do like Jessie's ma?"

Pa laughed. "That's the funniest thing I've heard in a long time."

"Then what were you up to, Pa?"

"Since we been here this past month, me and the boys have had a chance to see all the cattle and land your new in-laws have," Pa said. "But since Mrs. Kincaid doesn't seem to be keen on me, it is not likely I can get her into changing her last name. Which means…" Pa snickered, his tone lowered, kind of devious sounding. "I'm going to have to make other arrangements."

"What other arrangements?" Sarah didn't like the way he was acting right now. Greed filled his eyes, and Pa had a serious problem with greed, even worse than he had with gambling.

"Don't you worry about a thing, girl." Pa spat again. "You go back inside and enjoy time with that husband of yours while you can. We've got a lot of work to get done on the fencing tomorrow. Before any storms hit."

Sarah looked up at the orange and purples streaking through the sunset. Somehow, she figured Pa wasn't talking about the weather.

CHAPTER NINE

As much as they needed the rain, they didn't need mud slides, or cattle getting stuck. Jessie had told Caleb and Montana that he'd ride back and see if any of the ranch hands were back at the bunkhouse. They were already tending to their own set of problems because of the storm and flash flooding. Marshall had his own duties as sheriff which he was obligated to take care of before he could come help them out on the ranch.

Jessie tied his horse up to the post and hurried into the bunkhouse. Great. Of all the people he'd find, it had to be Sarah's pa and her brothers who were sitting at the table playing a game of checkers. The boys really weren't too bad when her pa wasn't around. But Jessie was still a tad irritated with the man for flirting with Ma at dinner. Thankfully, Ma was a level-headed woman and wouldn't be taken by the likes of a deceitful man like him, but Jessie had still talked with Sarah about it when they went to bed last night.

Sarah warned him to watch out for her pa. She told him she had a feeling her pa was up to something, but she didn't know what. Jessie promised to keep an eye out.

"I need you and the boys to help me rescue stray cattle." Jessie took his cowboy hat off. The water rolled off of it onto the rug that he was standing on near the door.

The boys looked hesitantly at their pa who was lying on his bunk, looking at a newspaper. No doubt the boys wanted to see if their pa would be agreeable to going out in the bad weather. To his credit, he nodded toward them and rose to his feet. Zeke and Elijah scooted their chairs back and stood.

"We're going to check down near the creek," Jessie said. "Caleb and Montana were around the northwest section land rescuing a cow that was stuck. Its calf wouldn't leave her and now it's stuck, too."

"You said we're going down by the creek?" Pa asked.

Jessie nodded.

"Ain't there chances of flash flooding around there?" Pa's eyebrow arched a fraction.

Jessie couldn't quite read his expression, 'because he thought the man almost sounded happy.

"A person could just about drown if they got washed away," Pa said.

"Yeah, and that creek is a lot deeper than most around these parts. That's why we built a wooden bridge across it. Too bad the animals didn't have the fool sense to use it to get out of harm's way in this weather." Jessie pointed toward the cabinet in the corner of the room. "Zeke, you want to grab a couple ropes out of that cabinet? Wouldn't hurt to make sure we all have one with us for safety."

Zeke did as instructed, and handed his brother and Pa a rope, keeping one for himself. Jessie already had one on his saddle. They headed out and rode down to the creek. Flashes of occasional lightning and thunder reverberating loudly through the open land made Jessie tremble. He'd heard tales of people being hit by lightning, and even one person's body burned beyond recognition. The quicker they got their tasks done, the quicker they could all get back inside and stay safe.

"Up ahead," Sarah's pa shouted, pointing up the creek near the wooden bridge. "There's a calf. Its ma is stuck on the other side."

They were on the same side as the ma. "Why don't you stay here with the cow, and I'll take Elijah with me across the bridge to get the calf. But we better hurry. This water is already lapping at the banks."

Pa nodded. "I'll come with you both. Zeke should be okay. It'll be quicker this way."

Jessie's lips pursed tight. He didn't want to stop and argue. Leaving the older boy alone with the cow wasn't something he felt akin to do, but it might be faster having the extra pair of hands. Jessie led the way.

Halfway across the bridge, Sarah's pa clasped his shoulder and pointed over the side of the bridge. "What's that in the water? I think it started to go under."

Jessie leaned over the edge, straining to look. The water was raging with the speed and strength of a river. Any person or critter that got caught up in the water was sure to be drowned. "I don't see anything."

"Maybe 'cause it hasn't happened yet," Pa shouted.

Jessie started to turn but lost his balance as his legs were hoisted out from under him. He shouted and ended up taking in a mouthful of water as his body went underwater. He fought his way back above the water, coughing as he came up for air.

Sarah's pa stood on the bridge watching Jessie's arms flail as he tried to fight to stay afloat. Her pa was holding Elijah's shoulders, keeping the boy back. It looked like Elijah wanted to help Jessie because he was wrestling in his father's arms.

"Hold on, Jessie."

Jessie looked to the side of the creek where he heard the shouts coming from. Zeke was running along the creek, trying to keep up with Jessie while he was making a lasso. At least the boys wanted to save Jessie. Thankfully, they weren't a part of their father's plan. And Jessie had a feeling this wasn't a last-minute idea he came up with either. Sarah's pa had been acting peculiar from the moment Ma put him in his place last night.

It took Zeke three attempts and throwing the lasso to Jessie before Jessie could grab on. He quickly wrapped it around his torso and tried swimming toward the creek bank. An undertow caught Jessie and pulled him under. He fought hard against the current. Once he was free of the water's undertow, he looked over toward shore, but no one was there.

"Help," Zeke shouted.

He must have fallen in when Jessie was pulled under. With even more determination, Jessie swam against the current to reach Zeke.

Elijah and Pa were at the bank of the creek when they reached the side. Their pa reached for Zeke's hand. Jessie struggled on his own to climb out of the water, his body weak from fighting the current. He could barely stand, let alone wring Sarah's pa's neck. Which is what he wanted to do. The fool man almost cost Jessie his life.

Jessie grabbed Pa's arm. "What in tarnation were you trying to do?"

Sarah's pa's response was a punch to Jessie's left cheek. Jessie squeezed him tighter, trying to keep his balance. The effort was futile, because Sarah's pa stumbled toward him and they both landed in the creek.

Jessie let go of him. The last thing he needed was for the man to hold him under water. He didn't have the strength to fight the man. As is, he'd be lucky to make it back to shore.

CHAPTER TEN

Jessie felt warm. His head hurt too much to open his eyes.

"Jessie?" Sarah squeezed his hand tight. Her voice sounded frantic.

Water. Drowning. Was Sarah all right? Jessie moaned as he struggled to open his eyes. The first thing he saw was his wife's face. She was crying. She did that too much. "Don't cry."

Sarah was sitting on a chair next to him on the settee. She leaned over and planted kisses all over his face. "Oh, thank goodness you're all right."

"You had us plum scared, Boy," Ma said.

"Thank goodness Jessie is a better swimmer than the rest of us." Jessie's gaze followed the sound of Marshall's voice.

Everyone was standing around him, and they were safe inside.

"How'd I get here?" Jessie strained to sit up.

"Don't get up," Ma said and handed Sarah another pillow to put beneath his head.

Jessie brought Sarah's hand up to his lips and kissed it. What he had to tell her wasn't going to be easy. But she needed to know. He'd also talk with his ma later about letting Sarah's brothers stay with them, but her pa had to go. Jessie didn't want that man around any of his family. "Your pa tried to kill me."

More tears trickled down her cheeks. Her dainty hands tightened around his. "I know. I'm sorry, Jessie."

"It's not your fault." Jessie strained to speak. All the creek water, he swallowed, must have irritated his throat. But he needed to finish this. "But we can't let him stay here any more."

Sarah closed her eyes and glanced away a moment. When she looked back at him, a single tear trickled down her cheek. "He won't be."

Jessie nodded, thankful that she agreed.

Ma moved next to Sarah and put her arm around her. She leaned down to kiss Sarah on the head, offering soothing words. "It will be all right, sweetheart."

"What's wrong?" Jessie looked at Ma, and then at his brothers. "What aren't you all telling me? Where's your brothers, Sarah?"

"They're at the bunkhouse," Ma told Jessie. "They are still shook up over their pa trying to kill you."

"If it wasn't for them," Marshall said. "You might have drowned."

"Elijah rode out to find us and told us you wouldn't wake up," Montana's voice was tense. "We were so afraid we'd lost you."

"I'm fine," Jessie assured them. He glanced at Sarah. She looked pale. "Where's your pa now?"

Everyone was silent. You could have heard a raindrop hit the ground as quiet as it was in the house. Marshall was the first one to break the silence. "He drowned, Jessie."

"I'm sorry, Sarah." Jessie struggled to a sitting position and hugged his wife. She melted into his embrace and cried. He rubbed her back and held her close until her sobs subsided. "It will be okay, sweetheart."

She sniffed and pulled back enough to stare into Jessie's eyes.

His insides ached at the pain he saw there.

"Pa got what he had coming to him," Sarah said. "But while I wanted to get away from him, I didn't want it to be like this."

"I understand." Jessie nodded. "But at least now your brothers may have a chance. If Ma and my brothers will help, we can be a better example for them to see the type of men they need to be and undo all the bad your pa instilled in them."

"I love you, Jessie." Sarah kissed his cheek and hugged him. "You're going to be a wonderful father."

"Thank you." Jessie smiled and whispered next to her ear, "I look forward to making babies with you."

Sarah's cheeks flushed, and she smiled. "Well, we've already made the first one. We just have to wait for it to get here."

It took a moment before her words registered with his foggy brain. "You're pregnant?"

Sarah bit her lower lip and nodded.

Jessie shouted in joy and pulled her close into his embrace. The sadness they felt for the loss of her pa could be dealt with later. Right now, was time to celebrate new life.

He claimed Sarah's mouth with his. The kiss he gave her warmed him inside in a good way. When the kiss ended, she was a little out of breath. He had to admit he liked having that effect on her. Jessie kissed her again, then trailed kisses down her cheek to her neck so he could whisper in her ear again. "Do you think maybe we could go practice making babies for a while?"

"If that will make you feel better," Sarah whispered in his ear.

"Oh, it will make me feel much better." Jessie slowly stood. Taking her hand, he led her away from the others.

"Where are you both going?" Caleb asked.

Marshall elbowed Caleb. "They're tired."

Caleb frowned. "But he's been asleep since yesterday."

Montana took his hat off and hit Caleb upside the back of the head with it. "Shut up, Caleb."

Everyone laughed.

"Good night," Ma said and winked at them. "Make sure my grand baby gets lots of rest."

Jessie laughed. "We will."

Mail Order Brides: Montana's Bride

By Susette Williams

CHAPTER ONE

House Springs, Missouri – June 1843

The letter in Montana Kincaid's saddle bag called out to him, itching to be read. He'd waited plumb near two hours and still hadn't gotten a moment of solitude since they'd left town. If his brother, Caleb, wasn't with him, one of their hired hands seemed to be close enough to watch his every move. Even out in the field, herding the cows in the south pasture, he wasn't alone. They'd be done soon and then he could make an excuse for riding back on his own. That would be the only time he would get to read his letter in private, at least before he went to bed that night.

Receiving mail was one of the few forms of entertainment available. The last thing Montana wanted was people being entertained at his expense. He hadn't told anybody that he had replied to an ad for a mail order bride. His letters from Mary were personal. Nobody needed to know about her yet, but him. Well, at least until he could persuade her to come to House Springs and become his wife. She'd indicated in her previous letters that she had some things to tend to and that she would come before Sarah's baby was due, which was in December.

Waiting nearly six more months seemed like an eternity—not that he already hadn't waited, given he was twenty-seven years old. How bad was it that his kid brother found a wife before he had? Sending for a mail order bride hadn't turned out too terribly bad for Jessie. Granted, Sarah's pa ended up dying, but that was his own fault. Montana learned from Jessie's mistakes and made sure to ask Mary all about her family when they began corresponding.

Mary Dobson lived with her aunt and uncle because she lost both her parents to Diphtheria when she was a little girl. Her aunt and uncle were set on marrying her off, but Mary hadn't taken to any of the suitors they had introduced her to thus far. She had confided that he was not the only man who had responded to her advertisement for a husband. While he worried she might not find him as appealing in person, the only thing that mattered at the moment to Montana was, she no longer wrote anyone else but him. He couldn't help but smile at that thought.

Would she look anything like he'd envisioned? She wrote that she had long, brown hair that she wore up except for when she went to bed. Then, she braided it. He told her he had brown hair too, and a mustache, which she said made her smile. She apparently liked mustaches and she didn't mind that his eyes were brown. The fact that she looked forward to seeing them in person stirred a yearning deep inside his chest.

Mary told him that her bright green eyes stood out against her pale skin and that she had a narrow face. He'd written back and told her that she would have plenty of opportunity to get some sun in Missouri, especially being fairly close to the river. He could take her out on a boat and go fishing. Ma didn't mind fishing, so he was sure Mary would enjoy it as well. At least she had agreed to give it a try.

"Are you daydreaming again?"

Montana startled. "Well, you ain't very good company, Caleb."

His brother laughed. "That I ain't. I was thinking about heading into town and playing some cards later. Wanna come?"

"Nah." Montana steadied his horse. "You know Ma doesn't like us gambling."

"What Ma don't know..." Caleb's words trailed off as he prodded his horse in the sides with boots and rode away. "See you at home."

When Montana was thinking of how many ways Ma would tan Caleb's hide, a sudden thought occurred to him. He was alone. Truly alone. No one could see the boyish grin that crept to his face as he dug into his saddle bag and retrieved Mary's letter. He took a whiff. Smelled of lilacs. No doubt she smelled of lilacs, too. One thing was for sure, he couldn't wait to find out.

Mary's handwriting was elegant, unlike his. It took Montana a lot of effort to write legible enough for Mary to read his letters. He hadn't had much need for writing since he got out of school. Given that he'd only gone to the eighth grade, it had been quite a while.

Montana turned the envelope over and carefully opened it to retrieve the letter inside. It read:

My Dearest Montana,

After everything you have told me about Jessie and his wife, Sarah, I feel I need to be honest with you. Earlier this year I had been corresponding with a potential suitor, Calvin Peters, to whom my aunt and uncle had introduced me. I had responded to his letters out of politeness and respect for my aunt and uncle. However, I came to feel uncomfortable with the nature of the letters he was sending me and wrote him two months ago to tell him I was not interested in pursuing marriage with him.

To my surprise, I received a letter from him today. In his letter, he seems somewhat confused. I thought I had made my intentions perfectly clear, but he insists that things would be different if he came here to see me again. I can assure you there is nothing that he could say or do that would convince me to change my mind.

I hope that you don't mind that I intend to come earlier to see you than we had previously discussed in our recent correspondence. As soon as I mail this letter, I will secure a seat on the stagecoach and should be leaving within a day or two.

I have given my friend a letter to give to Calvin Peters should he show up in Carson City as he has implied that those are his intentions. I do not wish to be here when he arrives. I fear he has become overly enamored with me to the point that I have become fearful.

Please know that I would never knowingly cause you any grief, and I will totally understand if you do not wish to see me upon my arrival. If you do, I hope that we will be able to be married soon. I am ready to begin a new chapter in my life.

All my affections,

Mary

Montana's fists tightened. He didn't want to accidentally scrunch the letter from Mary, but it was hard to loosen his grip when all he could think of doing was punching somebody. Calvin Peters to be exact. The man had best hope that he never crossed his path.

The only consolation was that Mary would be there soon. A clump formed in the pit of his stomach. There was one thing left to do—let Ma know that she'd have another daughter-in-law soon. Telling her couldn't be any worse than cleaning out a horse's stall. It might stink during the process, but it would be better once it was done and over with.

CHAPTER TWO

"You're what?" Ma glared at Montana from her wooden rocking chair in the living room. "Don't you think you should have told me about her well over a month ago?"

"Well..." Montana stuttered, wishing the couch would open up and swallow him whole. He never did like being on Ma's bad side. "I—"

"...definitely wasn't thinking," Ma finished her own version of what she figured he should have been saying. "We're supposed to get everything around here gussied up within a day or two?"

Montana fidgeted with his hat in his hands, nodding and making an apologetic face. What could he say?

"You know this home doesn't have a lot of feminine touches." Ma looked down at her trousers and then back toward Montana.

He knew what she was thinking. Ma didn't dress like other women. She dressed like a man because she worked as hard as one.

"When your pa died, I had four boys to raise while taking over the responsibilities of the ranch."

"I know, Ma. You've always been hard working and had to do the work of a man. We appreciate how good you've always looked out for us."

The frown lines around her mouth softened, a look of tenderness in her eyes. There wasn't much that softened Ma's exterior façade.

"I already talked with Mary and she knows what she's walking into and that life on a ranch is a lot of work." Montana didn't want Mary finding out any surprises, and he didn't want any either. That's why he'd made her promise to be honest with him from the beginning, and he would be, likewise.

"Who knows what they're walking into?"

Montana turned to see Marshall closing the door.

"Dinner smells good, Ma." Marshall sniffed. "Is that stew?"

"Yep. I even made some biscuits to go with it."

"Sounds good." Marshall hung his hat on the rack by the door and took a seat on the other end of the couch. Crossing his leg, he brushed off some dust from his boot. "So little brother, continue. I'd love to hear who *she* is and what she might be walking into."

"Don't you have some sheriff duties to tend to?"

"And miss out on this conversation?" Marshall chuckled. "The fact that you're trying to get rid of me tells me I'm right where I need to be."

"I think your brother would rather let me digest the news before he has to deal with you and the others ribbing him about his engagement," Ma said.

Marshall's attention darted from Ma to Montana, then he did a double take, checking to see if their expressions belied any sense of humor. "His engagement?"

Montana tossed his hat on the coffee table. He glared at his older brother. "There's nothing wrong with a man wanting to get married."

"Did you ever think that maybe you should meet her and get to know her first?" Marshall's eyes widened

~ 59 ~

momentarily as he gave Montana that, 'are you really that dumb' stare.

"We've been writing each other for a couple months and have gotten to know a lot about each other. Part of marriage is getting to know everything there is about the other person." While he and Marshall may have shared very similar facial features, except Montana only had a mustache, not a beard, the two of them were very different. Perhaps his brother's position had made him more cynical concerning people. He spent his days dealing with less than desirable elements. It was likely to have an effect on his view of people. "I feel confident that Mary is exactly the type of person she has portrayed in her letters."

"Yeah, cause people who write strangers, claiming they want to spend the rest of their lives with them is perfectly normal behavior and shows that you can trust them." If Marshall's facial contortions weren't enough, his comment was laced with obvious sarcasm. "Tell me, what convinced you more—the way she wrote each letter on the page, or perhaps you were too intoxicated by the perfume she scented each page with?"

Montana grabbed for his pocket, feeling to make sure Mary's letter was still there. "How did you know she used perfume on her letters?" If Marshall read any of them, Montana would surely be wanted for murder, because he'd kill his older brother for snooping where he didn't belong. "You didn't even know about Mary before you got here."

"I can smell the perfume." Marshall smirked. "Obviously you've been handling that letter a lot today."

Ma chuckled.

Heat rose in Montana's face. He couldn't refute Marshall's comments. They both knew Ma didn't wear perfume, and Sarah couldn't handle the smell of it in her current state.

"In all seriousness, little brother, I'm just worried about you." Marshall's expression sobered. "While things may have worked out for Jessie with Sarah, her pa did try to kill him. I would feel better if you let me do a little digging to see what I can find out about this woman and her family first."

Montana ran a hand through his hair. "It ain't her or her family that I'm worried about."

"You didn't mention you had any concerns." He didn't like the scowl on Ma's face.

"It isn't anything really," Montana said. "Mary's aunt and uncle introduced her to a potential suitor and she didn't feel anything for the fella, she only wrote him out of politeness to her kin. However, this fella does not seem to understand that when a woman says she ain't interested that it means she really doesn't want to see you again. He wrote and told her that he was on his way, so she is coming here. I figure the stagecoach may take a little longer than the mail to arrive, so it could be a day or two before she gets here."

"What's the name of this fella?" Marshall bit the one side of his lower lip, like he always did when he was thinking about a problem that needed to be solved. "I can ask around, see if anyone has heard of the guy."

Montana didn't need to look at Mary's letter. He wouldn't forget the guy's name anytime soon—definitely not before he and Mary got hitched. Once the man saw that she was married, he was sure to move on. "His name is Calvin Peters."

CHAPTER THREE

Montana paced in front of the stage depot, pausing only to check his pocket watch. They should have been here by now. Granted, he only cared about Mary, but his concern for her not showing grew when the whole stagecoach didn't show. It normally arrived a few hours before noon, and it was nearly four in the afternoon. Maybe he better get Marshall? They could ride out to see if they met up with them along the way.

Having settled things in his mind, Montana stepped down off the platform onto the dirt road and headed across the street for his brother's office. Being able to readily ask law enforcement to help, and knowing they'd actually do it, was one of the perks of having a brother as the sheriff.

Hillsboro was a small town in regard to population, but it became known as the county seat a little over a year ago. Which was beneficial to the town because it helped them to get the courthouse that they were currently building at the corner of Second and Oak Street. Not only would they get to have more holding cells to put criminals in, they would be able to prosecute them—no waiting for a judge to show up.

Montana entered the brick building. He nodded toward Marshall when he spotted him across the room, talking with another one of the deputies.

Marshall finished his conversation and came over to meet Montana. "What's up, little brother?"

Montana laughed. "You realize I'm only a year younger than you are?"

His slightly-older brother smiled. "And you're a couple inches shorter, making you my little brother no matter how you look at it."

They both chuckled.

"I'll give you that one." Montana sighed, his expression sobering at the remembrance of the reason for his visit. "Have you heard any news concerning the stagecoach?"

"No." Marshall shook his head as he sat on the edge of the desk. "You know something I don't?"

Taking his hat off, Montana ran a hand through his hair before putting his Stetson back on his head. Maybe he was overreacting? The only thing he knew was that he'd feel better when she was here—with him. "Mary is arriving today, and the stagecoach should have been here already. It's not like them to run so late, is it?"

"Hmm, not usually." Marshall leaned slightly to look past where Montana was standing. "Chase, you heard anything about the stagecoach?"

Montana turned so he could see Chase's face. He'd met him before—a nice man, he was a little on the lean side. Marriage agreed with his disposition, but apparently his wife had yet to master her cooking skills. At least Mary could cook, or so she said.

"There was a fella that rode into town this morning and said he'd passed the stagecoach. They were replacing a broken wheel," Chase said. "I'm sure they'll be here soon."

Montana tipped his hat toward the deputy. "Thank you."

"Not a problem." The deputy went back to looking at the papers on his desk.

"You wanna grab a bite to eat while you wait?" Marshall stood. "I could sure use the company."

He hated to make his brother eat alone. Even though he'd moved out a couple years ago, he often showed up for dinner. "You really ought to think about getting a wife."

Marshall let out a hearty laugh. "I said I wanted company, not a nag."

"What makes you think a wife will be a nag?"

His brother shrugged. "Seems women tend not to understand that law enforcement requires a flexible schedule. The bad guys don't seem to understand that crimes need to be committed sometime after breakfast and wrapped up in plenty of time so that we won't be late for supper."

"You don't know that a woman wouldn't be able to deal with your job." Montana thought about how many times he could remember hearing about Marshall having to go on a manhunt, some of which took him away for days on end. Ma was practically a saint, and even she'd complained. "How about I just get a cup of coffee? Ma's planning to have dinner ready when we get in."

"Sure, rub it in." Marshall patted him on the back as they headed toward the door. "You get Ma's roast."

"You can always come home for supper."

"If I didn't have to spend the night at the jail." Marshall opened the door and Montana followed him out. "A deputy's wife is having a baby, so I said I'd stay here tonight in his place."

They both turned at the sound of horses and the stagecoach passing by, stopping in front of the depot. Montana stopped and stared. The air caught in his lungs. His destiny awaited him.

"Looks like I'm doomed to eat alone tonight after all." Marshall nudged him, knocking him out of his trance. "Doesn't mean I can't at least meet my future kin."

Marshall stepped down, picking up his pace, he quickly cleared the distance between him and the stagecoach. Once it registered, Montana took off at a trot to catch up with him. "You better be on your best behavior, Marshall."

"Or what?" Marshall asked over his shoulder.

"Or she'll never marry me, and I'll end up moving in with you, making sure you become a miserable man as well."

"All right." Marshall chuckled. "You don't have to be so dramatic."

When they rounded the back end of the stagecoach, two women stood on the platform, both had brown hair. The younger, and prettier, one said, "Mary," when speaking with the other woman.

The older woman was Mary? Montana gulped and looked at Marshall, who was grinning from ear-to-ear. "Good luck little brother."

He glared at Marshall. Pasting a pleasant smile on his face, Montana approached both of the women, forcing himself to look at Mary, so she wouldn't be hurt by him gawking at the other beautiful woman. He reminded himself that it was her kind and loving spirit in her letters that had won him over. A peace settled over him as he thought about the letters she had been sending him over the last few months. With confidence, he approached them.

"I'm so glad you were able to make it." Montana extended his hand to Mary. "I was worried when your stagecoach hadn't arrived."

Mary took his hand. "That's very kind of you."

"I would like for you to meet my brother, Marshall."

To his credit, Marshall did not start laughing. He even did his best to school his enjoyment of the situation. "It is a pleasure to meet you, Mary."

"I'm sorry, I'm not Mary," she said.

The other woman's laughter sounded like music. Both men turned their attention to her. "It seems you have me confused with Mrs. Thompson."

Marshall stopped smiling, his mouth slightly agape.

Montana's spirits instantly soared. He said a silent prayer of thanks. His cheeks warmed when he remembered he was still holding Mrs. Thompson's hand. He let go. "I'm sorry for the confusion, ma'am."

She smiled. "Not to worry, dear. You made my day."

"And mine as well," Mary said, a gleam in her eyes.

CHAPTER FOUR

Mary smiled at the memory of Montana holding Mrs. Thompson's hand. She appeared genuinely flattered by his attention. The slightly older woman either had a hearing problem or tended not to listen very well. Mary had repeated her name to the woman on several occasions during their travel, and again when they were getting ready to part ways on the stagecoach depot platform. Mrs. Thompson had asked her name so that she could add her name to her prayers. While Mary would have been happy if Mrs. Thompson remembered to pray for her, Mary felt her prayers had already been answered the moment she saw Montana.

He was even more handsome than she imagined. His chocolate brown eyes and the way his mustache twitched when he smiled stirred a flurry of butterflies within her stomach. Her tummy hadn't settled during the course of their wagon ride thus far. She doubted it would until after they reached his family's homestead. She took the opportunity to observe Montana since she was seated next to him in the wagon. Their first time being alone, and he appeared to be every bit the gentleman he was in his letters. "I must confess, I was quite amused when we met."

Montana glanced at her momentarily, then focused his attention back on the road. "I am regretful for my behavior." His cheeks flushed. "When I heard you say 'Mary', I thought you were addressing her."

Mary covered her mouth in an attempt to hide her amusement. "I'm sorry." It was her turn to warm with embarrassment. "I can't help but laugh when I think of your expression and of your brother's when he found out that she wasn't me."

Loud guffaw erupted from Montana.

Mary loved how good-naturedly he took things. Her uncle had been a serious sort, always so stern-looking. Montana was refreshing, a true joy to be around. With him, Mary felt like she could be herself, not so prim and proper, as her aunt and uncle had expected. "I'm going to love being married to you."

Montana's expression sobered faster than a drunk who'd been dunked in a cold river. He glanced at her several times, trying to keep an eye on the horses and where they were going along the path. "I don't know whether I should stop the wagon and kiss you or what. My mind wants to think of something sweet to say in return, but I'm not good with flowery words." He slowed the horses to a halt and stared into her eyes. "All I can say is I am the luckiest man alive to be marrying a woman like you."

The air escaped her lungs with his heartwarming confession. His lips descended upon hers in a gentle kiss that both rejuvenated her senses and curled her toes. He caressed the side of her face in his palm while gently strumming his thumb across her cheek. The motion made her hunger more for his kiss. When he lifted his head, parting their lips, she swayed.

"What do you think about getting married Sunday after service?" His voice was low and sounded smooth as melted butter.

She blinked. "This Sunday?"

Flashing his pearly white teeth, he nodded. "Yes, there is a potluck dinner after church. It would be the perfect time to get married."

This Sunday? That was only four days away.

Montana nuzzled his nose next to hers. His lips mere inches from hers. Her lips parted. He feathered kisses against her lips, teasing and taunting her. "Wouldn't it be wonderful to do this all the time?"

Mary reached up and grabbed the back of his head, pulling it closer. She kissed him, not caring if her actions were proper. His teasing had driven her crazy with wanting. Come Sunday, she would have the pleasure of kissing him again, and that night, they wouldn't have to settle for just a kiss.

"Yes," the single word expelled like a gush of wind. "I'll marry you this Sunday."

He drew her close in his embrace, kissing the side of her head. "You don't know how happy that makes me."

She knew how happy it made her. If they didn't get back on the road shortly, she was likely to beg him to take her back into town and marry her tonight. "It might be best if we got on our way. I want to make a good impression on your family."

Montana winked at her and planted a kiss on her cheek before taking the reins back up between both hands and setting the horses back in motion. "I know they'll love you as much as I do."

Mary wrapped her arms around his bicep and leaned her head against his shoulder. "I love you, too."

"You keep that up and I'm gonna stop this wagon and kiss you again."

Giggling like a school girl, Mary looked up at him and smiled.

"Four days." Montana let out a frustrated sigh. "I just have to hold out for four more days."

CHAPTER FIVE

Ma turned out to be even more spectacular of a woman than Montana had made her out to be in his letters. It was no wonder he idolized her, because after getting up to make breakfast every morning, she helped with the cattle and the ranch. His mother was a remarkable, self-sufficient woman.

At least the previous three days, she had allowed Mary and Sarah to make lunch, when Sarah was not feeling under the weather due to being with child. Mary touched her own flat stomach and envisioned what it would be like to carry another life inside her. She smiled. Today was their wedding day. The Lord willing, she and Montana would be having their own little bundle of joy next year.

Ma had insisted Mary take the morning to get ready while Ma made a roast for the potluck dinner after church. Mary looked in the mirror and smoothed her cream-colored dress that she'd chosen to wear to church and for their wedding. She'd take extra care in fixing her hair up after having slept with it wrapped in cotton strips to curl it during the night. Taking a deep breath, she closed her eyes as the air slowly expelled from her lungs and calmed her nervousness.

Turning to head for the bedroom door, she paused when she looked at the bed. This was Montana's room, but he had been banished to Marshall's home until they were married. Tonight, it would truly become their room. Butterflies danced inside her tummy. The thought made her both nervous and excited. They had decided after exchanging affections on the way home that first night that perhaps it was best to wait until their wedding day to kiss again, lest they be tempted to sin. Montana confessed that he also had waited for marriage, which would make tonight special for both of them. With a smile on her face, she left the confines of the bedroom.

Mary spotted Montana from behind when she entered the living room. He spun around to greet her and paused, his mouth agape. In his hands, he held a beautiful mixed bouquet of flowers—roses, gardenias and stephanotis, from what she could tell. "Those are absolutely lovely."

Montana didn't respond. He just stood there.

Subconsciously, Mary reached up and touched the side of her head to adjust one of the loose curls. She smoothed her hands across the fabric of her dress before clasping her hands in front of her.

Jessie slapped Montana on the back and nodded toward Mary. "Say something."

"You look a whole heap prettier than these flowers." Montana's hand darted out in front of him with the bouquet clasped tightly in his grip. The flowers shook in the wake of the action, causing a few petals to tumble to the floor.

Caleb practically fell out of his chair laughing.

Montana flashed him an angry look.

His brother's smirk widened. "What you boys will do for your mail order brides." Caleb shook his head. "You won't catch me acting silly for any woman."

"Really?" Ma chuckled. "Seems I recall you getting pretty stung up climbing a tree to get to a bee hive for a girl you were sweet on when you were younger."

Caleb frowned and stood. "That was a long time ago. You won't catch me writing some woman I don't know and then pretending to be such a gentleman to please her." He headed for the door.

"That's 'cause you don't want any woman to see that you can't write," Montana quipped. "She'd be bound to like your perty pictures though."

Caleb slammed the door on his way out.

"Touchy fellow." Jessie gently patted Sarah's belly and kissed her on the cheek.

"Your brother is just upset because the two of you found women to make you happy and he doesn't have anyone," Sarah said.

"But Ma." Montana hiked a thumb over his shoulder in the direction of their mother.

"Oh, no way," Ma said. "That boy needs to get to get married and not live with me for the rest of his life."

Jessie began to sulk. "I'm married, and I live with you."

Ma pinched his cheeks in each of her hands. "That's because you gave me a beautiful daughter-in-law and my first grandbaby. If I let you leave I wouldn't get to see either of them nearly as much."

He grinned.

"Sounds more like she's holding you hostage." Montana chuckled. "Hopefully Mary and I will have our home built before winter."

Montana had moved next to her, his arm around her waist. She melted when he winked at her.

"Save it for later, you two. If we don't get out of here we will be late for church." Ma headed for the door, her dish for the potluck dinner wrapped in a couple of folded feed sacks so as not to burn her hands on the hot pot. "Get the door, Caleb. We've got a wedding to get to."

They all followed Ma outside. Sarah, Jessie and Ma rode in one wagon, while Montana and Mary rode in one by themselves. Caleb opted to take his horse—as if somehow riding with either of the couples might rub off on him and he might catch the 'marriage fever.'

Thankfully, they didn't have a very long ride to church. Mary continued to caress her flowers. She brought them up close enough to smell.

"You smell even better than they do." Montana glanced at her and winked. He'd winked at her several times in the past day or so. Their eyes had locked on numerous occasions. By the look in them, she knew he was thinking about kissing her because he'd continually glance at her lips and then when he looked back up he had a gleam in his eyes.

"I can't believe today is the day."

He threw a look her way. "You're not having second thoughts, are you?"

Mary wrapped an arm through his. "You can't get rid of me that easily."

His muscles relaxed. "Good. I plan to keep you around for a very long time."

"I sure hope so." Mary leaned her cheek against his shoulder. "Because I can't think of anywhere else I would rather be."

CHAPTER SIX

Montana looked at his pocket watch. The preacher seemed especially long-winded today. Perhaps the fact that he knew everyone would be staying around after church for the potluck dinner assured him of a captive audience.

"I know everyone is anxious to eat," Matthew Morgan said. "But I assume since Mr. Kincaid has glanced at his pocket watch three times since I began preaching, that he is in an extra special hurry."

The congregation laughed. While Montana felt a little embarrassed, he wasn't about to apologize for his impatience on his wedding day.

"His silly grin and the rosy color of his fiancée's cheeks are signs that I have indeed been a bit zealous today in my delivery of the Word." Matthew smiled. "Would you both do me the honor of joining me in the front so that we can commence with this wedding?"

Several people clapped. It didn't escape his notice that his youngest brother, Jessie, whooped and hollered. Today was a special day for celebrating, a day they would remember for the rest of their lives. Montana didn't mind that at least one other family member had verbally echoed the excitement he himself felt inside. Ma and his other two brothers should appreciate the fact that they would at least be able to attend his wedding—something that none of them were privy to with Jessie and Sarah's wedding.

Montana scooted out of the pew and waited for Mary to join him in the aisle before taking her smaller, delicate hand in his and walking down to the front of the church to meet the preacher. It took a great deal of concentration to keep his stride normal. If he'd taken steps as fast as his racing heart, he would have run down the aisle. While he was anxious to marry Mary, he wasn't prepared to drag her to the altar and make a spectacle of himself.

When they stopped in front of the preacher, Montana's heart continued to beat erratically. He glanced at Mary and something about the look of peace in her eyes transcended from her all the way clear through to his inner being. He'd loved her in her letters, and now that she was here, he loved her even more. A lifetime would never be long enough to spend getting to know everything about each other or waking up each morning and staring at her in disbelief that such a beautiful creature had agreed to spend the rest of her life with him.

Their gazes remained locked as the wedding ceremony proceeded and he vowed to love, honor and protect her so long as the two shall live. A few snickers sounded in the congregation when he'd said protect and the preacher said cherish. Montana looked at the preacher and quickly amended, "Oh, I'll definitely cherish her." Glancing back at Mary, he said, "All the days of my life."

Mary smiled and giggled, while a few women in the congregation let out sounds of awe.

No sooner had the preacher pronounced them man and wife, he took the opportunity to kiss his wife. She smelled of lilacs, just like her letters. He vowed to one day start her a garden, after they built their new home, then she would always have flowers to put in their home and it would smell as heavenly as she did.

"Now that the Kincaids are married, let's all head out back for vittles and we can celebrate their happy union," Pastor Morgan said.

Marshall was one of the first to congratulate them. He clasped Montana's shoulder. "I know the two of you will be happy together. You're getting a good husband, Mary. My brother will always look out for you and be a good provider."

"I know he will," Mary said. "Your ma has done a fine job of raising all of you boys."

Warmth filled Marshall's eyes. "That she did."

"Did someone mention me?" Ma asked.

"I was telling Marshall that you've done a wonderful job of raising your boys. They're all very hardworking and responsible men. You've got a lot to be proud of." Mary hugged Ma.

Ma's eyes misted.

"Are you crying, Ma?" Montana couldn't remember a single time Ma had ever cried about anything—except Pa's death, but that was a sad occasion.

"Don't be silly." Ma playfully slapped him against his arm with the back side of her hand. "I'm not the pouty sort."

In a rare display of affection, Marshall wrapped an arm around Ma. "No, but if you want to show a soft side, your boys won't think any less of you. Remember, you are our Ma too, even if you've had to fill Pa's shoes all these years."

Ma laughed. "Pa always said he chose a strong woman as his wife because traveling out west before it was very populated was a hard task. We covered some rough terrain on our travels."

"So, you haven't always lived in Missouri?" Mary asked.

"No. Why don't I tell you more about it over lunch?" Ma smiled and wrapped her arm through Mary's, leading her toward the door. Montana and the rest of their family followed. "Montana actually got his name from our time spent passing through there."

"Was he born there?" To his dismay, Mary seemed genuinely interested.

"Ma, you don't have to tell her how I got my name."

"You're right," Ma said. "But I'm going to anyway."

Montana heard his brothers' boisterous laughter ring out as they stepped outside and headed around to the back of the church. His brothers were thoroughly enjoying this tale at his expense.

"As I was saying," Ma continued. "He was conceived in Montana."

Mary covered her mouth, her eyebrows raised as she glanced over her shoulder at him. "Oh, my."

"Thanks, Ma. Not something my new bride needed to hear."

"Well, if you're lucky," Ma said over her shoulder, "she won't let you name your first son Missouri."

"Mary doesn't need to worry about that." Montana's tone sounded a bit sharp in his own ears. He took a deep breath. "I'm gonna name him Graysen, after Pa."

"What if we only have girls?" Mary asked. "After all, your Ma only had boys. God might see fit to only give us daughters."

Montana hadn't thought about that. Ma hadn't raised daughters, and didn't have any until Jessie and then he got married. Who would've thought a year ago that the two of them would have wives, and Jessie's wife with a baby due to be born by the end of the year. "I confess, I hadn't given any real thought to a girl's name. Maybe we could call her Graylee. Then she'd still sort of be named after her grandpa."

"That's a lovely idea." Mary stepped away from Ma's side and turned to him, planting her soft lips against his cheek in a heartwarming kiss. Mary turned to Ma and whispered in her ear. Ma nodded and pointed. "I'll return shortly, I promise."

Montana's heart beat quickened. "Do you want me to go with you?"

"No, thank you. That won't be necessary." Her smile should have been comforting, but he didn't like the thought of her not being by his side.

Once she was out of sight, he asked Ma, "Where did Mary need to go?"

"Woman stuff," was all Ma responded.

His cheeks warmed when he realized what Ma meant. He'd have to learn to be more sympathetic to a woman's needs now that he was married. Ma was a great woman, but she wasn't delicate like Mary.

CHAPTER SEVEN

Mary hoped she would never have to relieve herself in town again. The vapors had nearly overwhelmed her. Perhaps it was so nauseating because of the amount of use in town. Her uncle prided himself on keeping up with the newest inventions since he wished to invent things himself as well. He'd told her of a water closet and how they would eventually be available in towns and maybe even homes. While maybe a wishful dream of the future, she would have relished the thought of using one today. In the future, she would limit the amount of tea she consumed before traveling.

Glancing around, Mary tried to remember which direction she needed to go to get back to the church. Other than the day she arrived in Hillsboro on the stage coach and headed through the more populated part of House Springs on their way back to the Kincaids' settlement, she hadn't visited the town.

She took off in the direction from where she heard the most noise, assuming that it would most likely be coming from the gathering at church, she walked toward the mercantile, intent on making it back to the main street. As she passed an out-building behind the mercantile, a hand clasped around her arm and yanked her backwards as the man's other hand covered her mouth to keep her from screaming. He didn't feel like a large man, but he was stronger.

"Stop," he ground out in a low voice. "I have a gun and won't hesitate to use it if necessary. In fact, I'm half tempted to make you a widow right now."

Something about the voice made her shiver and so did his threat. But he said he'd make her a widow, not her husband a widower. Mary stopped struggling.

His grip eased a fraction. "If I take my hand off your mouth, do you promise not to scream?"

Mary nodded.

He let go of her arm, keeping his hand across her mouth. A second later, something hard pressed into her side. "I never intended you any harm, but you forced my hand by running off with this cowboy. If you squeal or draw any attention to us, I'll have no choice but to shoot, and trust me, if any of your in-laws make the mistake of crossing my path, I'll make sure they regret the day they met you."

Before his hand lowered from her lips and she'd even turned to look over her shoulder, she recognized the voice as her stomach sunk like a lead weight. Calvin Peters.

"I left a letter for—"

"I know what you left for me." Calvin put his arm around her waist securely, hiding the gun's barrel behind her. "You didn't have the decency to discuss things in person with me."

With her arm at her side, it wasn't likely anyone would see the gun handle. It was probably better that way, then nobody was likely to get hurt. When she left the note, she hadn't considered his feelings, only her own. It was understandable that Calvin was upset. Perhaps she could reason with him. After all, he was an educated man, not some wild savage. At least she hadn't gathered that from the things her aunt and uncle had told her about him before they began corresponding. They hadn't told her he was a few years older than she was. Considerably older given that he was balding on top of his head. "I'm sorry I didn't consider your feelings. Could we maybe just go somewhere and talk about this?"

"That's exactly what we're doing now." Calvin pressed her closer to his side. "Smile for the nice couple," he said as they were approaching a young couple, the woman obviously with child by the bulging tummy upon which she rested a hand.

He wouldn't hurt them—would he? She thought about Sarah and Jessie before relenting. Mary forced a smile and nodded at the couple, as did Calvin. His stained teeth and smirk repulsed her. She reminded herself, she had to remain calm so that everyone else would stay safe.

They stopped by a wagon at the far end of the mercantile. "Climb up and scoot over."

She did as instructed. Her eyes skimmed the area, silently hoping Marshall would make an appearance. If Montana showed up, it might only serve to agitate Calvin more, and he might make good on his promise. At least with Marshall being sheriff, she could only hope that Calvin would respect the position. "You do realize my brother-in-law is a sheriff?" She didn't wait for Calvin to respond. "If you let me go, or at least put the gun down while we all talk this out, I'll see to it that no charges are pressed against you."

"If you think you're going to hide behind him or his brother, think again." Calvin glared at her. He reached for the reins and set the horses off in the direction opposite the church. "Last I heard, sheriff's bleed, too."

CHAPTER EIGHT

"Shouldn't the missus be back by now?" Caleb asked. "She didn't run off on you, did she?"

Montana wasn't sure if Caleb was joking or being serious. Those same thoughts had plagued his mind for the last fifteen or twenty minutes. He'd checked his pocket watch several times and his stomach was growling since he was waiting to eat until his wife joined him. Hopefully there would be plenty of food left. Deputy Chase had already been back for food twice. The only reason he showed up at church today was for Montana's wedding and free food. A handsome wife was a good thing to have during a cold Missouri winter, but a woman who could cook was essential to a man's survival. Thankfully, Montana knew Mary could cook because Ma had allowed her and Jessie to use the kitchen to make lunch the last few days.

He glanced around once more and upon not seeing his wife, he looked across the table that they were sitting at, hoping Ma would oblige. "Ma, do you think you could go check on Mary? She may need feminine advice."

"Perhaps I should go." Sarah stood. "Maybe I can help calm any jitters she may be having. In case she's nervous about tonight."

"What's to be nervous about, she's already walked down the aisle and stood in front of the whole church," Caleb said. "If that don't make you nervous, nothing will."

Marshall ribbed Caleb in the side and they all laughed when the look of dawning registered on Caleb's face. His cheeks turned rosy and it wasn't from the light breeze.

Ten minutes later, Montana was frustrated by the well-wishers who'd come to congratulate him and his bride because they seemed more interested in speculation concerning her absence than congratulating them. His spirits brightened the moment he spotted Sarah coming back, until he realized that she was alone. Where was Mary? His heart pounded in his chest. Had she decided she didn't want to be married to him after all?

He got up from the picnic bench, taking large strides to close the gap between himself and Sarah. "Where is she?" He couldn't help the panic in his voice.

"I don't know." Frown lines creased Sarah's brow. "I asked several people if they had seen her and came across a couple who said they passed someone fitting that description with a man who was maybe four inches taller than I am and going bald. She saw them in front of the mercantile." Sarah glanced back toward the way she'd come. When she looked at Montana, her eyes held concern. "The woman said they both smiled, but not the kind of smile that was real. She said you can normally tell how sincere someone is by their eyes, and if anything, she said, the woman's expression seemed concerned."

"You said the guy was balding?" Montana asked.

Sarah nodded.

"Do you know if he was thin?" Montana's stomach tightened in knots.

"I think so." Sarah shook her head. "She said he had his arm around her, drew her real close to his body. She said, once she thought about it—it didn't look like a very romantic embrace."

"Calvin Peters." Saying the name was worse than swallowing cod liver oil. If he'd eaten, he would have expelled the contents of his food. "The guy who wouldn't stop writing to her or take no for an answer."

"I haven't heard back anything yet from my contacts." Marshall turned, his eyes scanning the crowd. When he spotted his deputy, he called him over to where they where they were all standing. "We need to round up a posse."

"What for?" Chase's eyes narrowed, his deputy persona kicking in. "Who are we going after?"

"My sister-in-law is missing." Marshall removed his cowboy hat, long enough to run a hand through his hair and place the hat securely back on his head. "A man named Calvin Peters—"

Deputy Chase cut Marshall off from being able to finish saying what he was saying, "The guy you were waiting to hear back from someone in St. Louis about. I meant to tell you we got word late last night. Seems he has a reputation for being violent with women. The way your friend talked, he's controlling with women because he's too weak to stand up to any man, but the problem is, they haven't been able to get any women to testify against him yet."

"I'll kill him if he so much as laid a hand on Mary." Montana clenched his fists.

Marshall laid a hand on Montana's shoulder. "Don't worry, we'll get Chief Rainwater to help us track him."

"On my way, Sheriff," the deputy said. "I'll be back shortly."

"Meet us outside the mercantile," Marshall shouted to Chase's retreating form. He turned to Montana. "Let's get a posse together." Marshall patted Montana's back. "We'll find her, little brother. I promise."

CHAPTER NINE

"We've been traveling for hours." Mary fanned her face with her hand. Driving along the water's edge reminded her how parched she was. "It's hot and I'm thirsty."

Calvin reached over the back of the seat and grabbed a canteen. "Here, this will do you."

After removing the lid, she wiped off the rim and took a sip. "What waterway is this?"

"It's the Miaramigoua River."

Mary wasn't familiar with that river, or wherever they were. How would she ever find her way back to civilization? She'd been trying for hours to get Calvin to stop, hoping she could find someone to help her get away from him. By now, her husband and his family would know she was gone. Hopefully her brother-in-law would send people to look for her. Unless they thought she got cold feet and ran out on Montana. Her heart felt like a lead weight in her chest. Surely, they wouldn't think she would do such a thing to her new husband? She loved him and would never willingly leave him—except to keep him and his family safe.

"I feel faint." Which was true. She didn't know if it was from the sinking feeling that no one may be coming to rescue her or because she didn't eat. "I only had a biscuit with jelly on it for breakfast."

Calvin glanced at her. His scowl more than conveyed his displeasure with her. "If I'd known you were gonna up and marry some fella the day I got to town, I would have stocked my wagon with supplies."

"I told you in my letter that I was going to marry someone else." Mary sighed. No amount of talking had gotten through Calvin's thick head yet that she was never going to marry him or even considered marrying him. "The only reason I ever wrote you in the first place was because my aunt and uncle wished me to, not because I wanted to."

"And since you've been in their charge since you were a child, you were doing what they wanted you to do."

"Exactly," Mary said, a spark of hope flickered.

"And you'll continue to do as they wish, which is to marry me." Calvin's smile was sinister, sending a frightening shiver coursing through her body.

"I'm already married."

"Well, if you ask me, you'd make a much better widow than being married to that guy." Calvin glanced at her long enough to wink. "I can assure you I will be a much better provider."

"You sure haven't shown that," Mary's replied in a curt tone. "I feel faint and you've refused to take me to any of the local towns so that we can get food." *And I can get away from you*, she silently added in her head.

"Quit your bellyaching," Calvin grumbled. "I'll take care of you."

Releasing the breath she hadn't realize she'd been holding, relief flooded her and she almost smiled at the glimmer of hope.

Nearly an hour later, the flames of anticipation quickly vanquished when she saw the rocks and an opening to a cave. "I thought you were taking me to find food."

Calvin snickered. "Like I'm going to risk you trying to get away."

"I wouldn't." Mary crossed her index finger over her heart all the while praying, asking God to forgive her this one simple lie.

Grabbing a handful of her hair, Calvin pulled her head closer to him, making her wince in pain. "You honestly think I'm going to fall for that?"

Mary tried to keep calm, hoping Calvin would settle back down. Since he'd kidnapped her, she'd discovered that the smallest of things set him off on tangents. "Fall for what?"

"You think you are the first woman to try running away from me?" Calvin scooted to the edge of his seat and climbed down, forcing her to follow by the hold he still had on her hair. "I can promise you, you'll be the last one that ever gets away from me."

There were others, was all she could think about. How did her aunt and uncle not know what a horrid man this was? She'd seen two sides of him today. It was like a good side warred with an evil side of him and at the moment it was obvious which side was winning. She didn't know what to say, so she said nothing for fear of setting him off. A tear slowly rolled down her cheek. It was too hard to turn her head to hide it from him since he was clutching her hair so tightly in his fist. As he drug her around to the back side of the wagon, she swiped away the tear with her hand while he was searching for something under a blanket. Her eyes widened when he pulled some rope out from the back of the wagon. Another tear threatened to trickle.

"Tears don't work on me," Calvin said. "Save them for your husband's funeral."

Several tears escaped her eyes. Her voice and words escaped her—there was no reasoning with this fanatical man.

Calvin forced her to follow him into the cave where he sat her down on the cool stone floor, then he bound her hands and feet.

"You don't have to do this," Mary pleaded. "Can't you take me with you?"

"Perhaps one day." Calvin stared at her, as if he was searching her very soul. "When you forget about that other fella and you come to love me."

CHAPTER TEN

It was getting later, in an hour or two the sun would be setting. Marshall didn't want to think of what Calvin might do or might have already done to Montana's wife. They had to find her and find her soon.

The trail was hard to pick up when they came upon the river. That was why they decided to split up and cover more ground quickly. After passing the covered bridge on the Meramec, Marshall opted to head for the town, hoping someone might have spotted them. Montana, along with a couple other men, Jessie and a Shawnee Indian guide decided to see if they could pick up the trail along the river.

Marshall tramped up the steps of the mercantile and headed inside to talk to the store owner. The store smelled of licorice. "Have you seen any strangers, the guy is about this high?" Marshall held his hand out, palm down, indicating around his shoulder height. "He doesn't have a lot of hair on his head. He was seen traveling in a wagon with a pretty little gal with brown hair. She was wearing a fancy white dress—cause she just got married today."

If the store owner had been thinner, he could have fit the general description that Marshall gave of Calvin. He wished he would have had a wanted poster or something to go by, even a picture of Mary to show the store owner would have been nice. Chances were, they didn't get a lot of visitors out here, so if he'd seen anyone, he was likely to remember them.

"Check down the street at the saloon," the storekeeper said. "A guy fitting that description came in here and got a few supplies. He asked about a place he could get some grub and I sent him down there."

"Mighty obliged." Montana tipped his hat to the man and headed back out of the mercantile to where the other men were outside with the horses. He scanned the surroundings, spotting the saloon. "The owner said someone fitting Calvin's description headed on over to the saloon. I want you all to be careful. We don't know if he has a gun."

"If he does, we'll shoot him," Caleb said. "Any man who nabs a woman, especially on her wedding day, ain't worth the ground he'll be buried in."

Other men in the posse echoed the same sentiments.

"We're here to arrest him if possible," Marshall said. "We're not a lynch mob and the law is the law. He's entitled to a trial." Although, even he had to admit, if they caught Calvin with Mary—it was a done deal—he was guilty!

They rode over to the saloon, Marshall noted there were a couple wagons within close vicinity. He instructed Deputy Chase to go around back in case he tried to make a getaway.

Caleb followed Marshall inside. When they spotted a balding man at the bar, Caleb stepped forward, but Marshall held his hand out in front of him. "Let me handle this." He didn't see any sign of Mary. "We need him alive—Mary's not with him."

His brother nodded.

Marshall closed the gap between them, stopping three feet from the man, he leaned against the bar. "Howdy."

The man glanced at him and nodded.

"Smells like some good food you got there."

"Sure hope so," the man said.

"My name's Sheriff Marshall." He watched the man's reactions carefully, lest he have to respond to any sudden movements. The man brandished a revolver in his holster. "What's your name?"

"Jeremiah Jones."

"Did you come to town alone?" Marshall asked.

"Yep, all by my lonesome." Jeremiah gathered the napkin the barkeep had given him full of food. "Any reason you're taking such an interest to a man like me?"

"As a matter of fact, my sister-in-law was kidnapped by a man fitting your description today."

Jeremiah nodded toward Caleb. "Is this here your brother?"

"Yeah." Montana noticed Jeremiah's eyes squint a fraction, but the sun was shining into the bar near where he stood so he couldn't read anything into the guy's expression. "He's not the one who's married, though."

"Maybe some day, young fella." Jeremiah winked at Caleb and tipped his hat as he passed by. "Sorry about your other brother's new bride. Hope you find her."

"Thanks," Caleb said. "Where to now, Marshall? Wanna ask some of the other locals?"

"Hold up." Marshall walked to the saloon doors and watched as Jeremiah climbed up on a horse and rode out toward the direction they had come. He didn't have a wagon, was traveling alone, and he headed in the direction toward House Springs. "I was hoping it'd turn out to be him."

Marshall gripped the wooden door tight with one hand and slammed the palm of his other hand against it. He wanted to hit someone. Why couldn't they find her?

"We'll locate Mary." Caleb put a hand on Marshall's shoulder. "Why don't we ask around in here and then we can spread out in town and talk to the other locals?"

Marshall nodded. They asked around, trying to describe someone they'd never seen before and then the lovely Mary, who was easy to describe. Something about Jeremiah Jones still niggled him in his craw. As they joined the others outside, it suddenly dawned on him. "I never said Mary was his new bride."

Caleb looked at him cockeyed. "What are you talking about?"

"Jeremiah said he was sorry about our other brother's new bride—I never said she was his new bride—just that my sister-in-law was kidnapped."

♥ ♥ ♥

"Wagon tracks lead to them caves," Montana's Indian guide said. He nudged Montana's arm and pointed. "There is wagon."

"Jessie, you take a couple men and head down that way." Montana motioned toward the direction he wanted them to go. "I'll take the others and head around the other way. Let's be quiet. I don't want to spook him and have him do anything that might hurt Mary."

"If I get a clear shot to take him out," Jessie said. "I'm taking it."

"I wouldn't expect anything less, little brother." He may have been Montana's little brother, but he'd done a lot of growing up this past year. It was hard to believe Jessie was twenty-four, married and had a baby on the way. Montana ushered up a prayer that they'd all make it home tonight, safe and sound, and with Mary.

A lone rider barreled in, climbing down off his horse. He tied it up next to the other horse, walked past the wagon and disappeared from sight. Montana's heart pounded in his chest the closer he and the other men got to the cave. All the men had their guns drawn as they edged ever closer. Outside an opening to the cave, he strained to listen. He scrunched down and eased his head around enough. He saw a man fitting the description Mary had given him of Calvin. He couldn't just shoot a stranger in the back. What if it wasn't Calvin?

Something or someone was on the ground under a blanket. Montana couldn't tell if it was her or not because the man was scrunched down, blocking his view.

"You're going to have to eat on the trail," the man said. "We need to keep moving."

The horses startled, drawing the man's attention. When he stood and turned around, Montana saw her— Mary. Sensing something was wrong, Calvin drew his gun.

Montana straightened. Everything in his being wanted to shoot Calvin for what he'd done, but Marshall was the sheriff and for that reason alone, Montana decided to give Calvin a chance. "You're surrounded, Calvin. Come out with your hands up."

"Time to make you a widow," he shouted, firing two shots in Montana's direction.

Montana ducked behind the stone wall of the cave's exterior. He couldn't risk bullets ricocheting off the walls and accidentally hitting Mary. "Don't shoot unless I'm hit," Montana ordered the other man with him, who nodded.

Montana took off running and dove, firing midair at Calvin—three shots in succession, all hitting the man in the chest as Montana's body cascaded down hard against the stone floor. The thud sent a ripple of pain clear through him, knocking the wind out of him.

"Make sure that guy's dead," Jessie shouted over his shoulder to one of the men in the posse. He holstered his gun, leaned over and extended his hand to help Montana up. "Way to go."

"Thanks." Montana put his pistol in his holster as well and ran over to Mary. Tears stained her cheeks. Calvin had bound and gagged her. Montana carefully untied her and removed the gag.

Her arms flew around his neck. "I was afraid I'd never see you again," she cried. "He told me if I didn't go with him quietly, he'd make your family hate me by making me a widow. I couldn't let him hurt you or the others."

The guy kicked Calvin's body. He didn't move. "He's dead."

Good, was the only thing that ran through Montana's mind. At least Mary would never have to worry about him coming after her again, and Calvin could never hurt another woman again either.

Any traces of insecurity Montana felt, that she may have realized she didn't want to be married to him, vanished. He wiped her tears with his thumbs while caressing her face. "Are you okay? Did he hurt you, Sweetheart?"

She shook her head. "I'm fine. Just hungry and I want to go home."

"Calvin grabbed some food back at the saloon. There oughta be something there for her to eat." Montana turned when he heard Marshall's voice. "Check that red and white napkin."

"Glad you could finally join us." Montana winked at Marshall.

"Well…" Marshall took his hat off and ran a hand through his hair before returning it to his head. "Truth be told, we ran into Calvin in town, but I wasn't sure it was him. He didn't have a wagon and was on his own."

"How'd you figure it out then?" Montana asked while opening the napkin and handing a biscuit to his wife.

"Thank you," Mary said and took a big bite. "Can I have some of that chicken, too? I haven't had lunch or dinner."

"You can have anything you want." Montana smiled and handed her a chicken breast, which she laid in her lap and began picking at. He turned back to his older brother. "You were saying?"

"He said something about your new wife and I never mentioned you just got married, just that your wife was abducted."

"I'm just happy I have her back, safe and sound." Montana leaned over and kissed his wife's cheek. His stomach gurgled.

Mary giggled and held out a piece of her chicken breast for him. "Sounds like you're hungry, too. Do you want a bite?"

"I'd like nothing more than to nibble on your neck." He winked at her and leaned over, taking the bite she offered, never taking his eyes off of her. "I hope you realize I'm never going to let you out of my sight again."

"Good." She smiled. "Now do you think we could head home?"

"You bet." He planted a peck against her lips before helping her stand. Leaning close to her ear, he whispered, "I do believe you owe me a wedding night Mrs. Kincaid."

"I owe you a lot of things, Mr. Kincaid." Her lashes fluttered. "And I will gladly repay you my debt of gratitude."

He smiled. "I look forward to it."

"Do you mind if I sleep in the back of the wagon on the way home? I'm feeling very tired." Mary yawned. She winked at him. "I'd like to be well rested."

"Jessie," Montana shouted.

"Yeah?"

"Let's get that wagon hooked up. Make sure to tie the extra horses to the back. You're driving the wagon home while I keep an eye on the misses."

Mail Order Brides: Caleb's Bride

By Susette Williams

CHAPTER ONE

House Springs, Missouri —July 1843

Caleb Kincaid didn't fancy playing cards in the saloon, amidst the inebriated stench and overly ripe smell of Jacob Sinclair. At least tonight, Caleb had the good fortune of sitting across from Jacob at the poker table, so the stench wouldn't be so potent.

He was having a hard-enough time enjoying himself after the confrontation he had with Ma on his way out the door. She didn't approve of him playing poker. Normally, he would have found something else to do on a Friday night, but since Jessie and Montana got married, they wanted to spend time with their wives or get together with other couples. What was a single man to do? Play poker. With other single men. Glancing at the other four men at the table, he could understand why they were single—and not just because there was a shortage of women out west, or in the Midwest.

"So, tell me, Jacob, how come a man your age never got married?" Caleb figured the man had to be close to sixty. The gruff beard, worn cowboy hat and the fact that he kept spitting tobacco and downing whiskey didn't make him look like too much of a prize. Perhaps getting his goat would get him riled up enough to get overconfident and he'd slip up. Nothing wrong with having a little fun and taking home some money tonight. "Reckon cards was the only thing you could get your grubby little hands on."

"Don't you worry about what I got my hands on, young feller," Jacob said. "I buried one wife and I'm about to bury—marry another."

"You're a widower?" Caleb couldn't hide his surprise.

"Yep."

"And you're getting married again?"

Jacob nodded. "You gonna play or keep asking me questions all night?"

Caleb called, not wanting to seem overly anxious. He needed another club, which he got as they were dealt their last card. It took everything within him not to smile and give away his good hand. He forced a frown, hoping to mislead his opponents.

Jacob took the bait. Adding his money to the center pot, he also tossed in a stack of letters and snickered. "I raise, and I'll even toss in my bride-to-be."

"All in," Caleb said, anxiously pushing the rest of his money to the center of the table. He smiled. "What do you mean you'll toss in your bride-to-be?"

"Too rich for my blood." The man next to him folded, tossing down his cards.

"It means I plan on winning. But if any of you varmints win the pot, you get my mail order bride as well."

Caleb's eyes widened. "Wait a minute. I didn't sign up for no wife."

Jacob smiled and reached for the pot. "Then it looks like you're folding. Not that you'd have won anyway."

Caleb's hands came down on top of Jacob's. "Hold it, old timer. I ain't said nothing about folding."

The old man looked him in the eye for several moments before nodding and drawing his hands away from the pot.

There were only three hands that could beat Caleb's full house—a straight flush, four of a kind, or another full house with higher cards. The odds were in his favor. Tossing his money into the center of the table with the rest, Caleb said, "What do you have?"

Grungy teeth surfaced when Jacob smiled. "I've got a flush, ace high."

A long, steady breath slowly escaped Caleb's lungs in a sigh of relief. He hadn't realized he'd been holding his breath. Even though he knew he should never gamble more than he could afford to lose—he'd been willing to risk a little more tonight to settle the restlessness within his soul. Caleb knew his lips had formed that lopsided grin, his brothers always said would get him in trouble, 'cause Jacob's smile faded, and his fists balled up as Caleb laid down his cards. "Full house, queens over tens, partner."

Caleb scooped his winnings closer and began sorting the money. It was a favorable night. He did well.

"Double or nothing," Jacob ground out between clenched teeth.

"Sorry, old man. Time to get out while the getting was good." Caleb stuffed his winnings into his pockets. He glanced at Jacob and held up the letters the man had added to the pot. "Besides, you don't seem to have anything left to bet."

Caleb was about to toss the letters to Jacob, more than happy to let him keep his fiancé, but before he had the chance to speak, a redheaded spitfire wearing a light green dress came crashing into the saloon, bellowing out the man's name. She was closer to Caleb's age, definitely younger than Caleb expected, and certainly a lot prettier than the type of woman he would have expected Jacob to be able to snag.

"Jacob Thomas Sinclair, what in tarnation do you think you're doing in the Devil's playhouse?" She had her hands planted firmly on her hips, cornering him with a pointed look.

It was too hard to resist chuckling at Jacob cowering beneath her angry glare.

"Do you find something amusing?" She flashed her volatile eyes toward Caleb. "Like the fact that on the eve of my wedding, my so-called fiancée is gambling away all of his money and I'll likely have to take in laundry if I hope to eat the rest of this month?"

Heat rose to his cheeks and his throat constricted— like he'd just eaten hot chili peppers. He tried to swallow so he could respond, but his mouth was drier than the desert. He wasn't giving her back the money he'd won, but if what she said was true, he'd make sure to give Matthew money to take food over to them. The preacher would make sure no one knew it was him. Ma always said, giving should be done in secret, like the Bible said. Then you'd get your reward in Heaven and no one felt like they owed you nothing and they kept their pride intact. Caleb extended the handful of her letters toward her.

She snatched them out of his hand, her anger once again focused on Jacob as she held them inches from his face. "What is a total stranger doing with my letters?"

"That there total stranger," Jacob said, nodding toward him, "is your new fiancée."

She looked at Caleb and for once, she was speechless. Caleb wished she'd stay that way. A flash of something flittered in her expression, too quickly to register within his frazzled brain. Before his jumbled thoughts came into focus and he could protest Jacob's statement, her shoulders straightened, and she had once again gained her composure.

"I hope you realize that as my husband, you will not be frequenting such questionable establishments again in the future?" Her left eyebrow arched. She clasped the letters close to her bosom, obviously looking at him for a response.

"Ma'am," Caleb stuttered and looked at Jacob. "I wouldn't dream of coming between you and Jacob."

"Did Jacob offer my hand in marriage to whomever won the pot?" she asked.

He nodded and stood, tilting his hat back slightly. "I assure you I told him I wasn't looking to take nobody's fiancé."

"I see." She smiled. "And yet you stayed in the hand?"

"Yes, ma'am." His cheeks warmed.

"So, then you won my hand in marriage fair and square." She turned to go and paused when she realized no one was following her. "Come along. It's time we head home and as I mentioned, should you find yourself tempted to patronize such an establishment again, keep in mind that 'until death do we part' doesn't necessarily mean old age."

CHAPTER TWO

Go out for a quiet night on the town—that's all he wanted. A little fun and conversation with some of the men in town. A reminder of how his night really went had two arms wrapped around his midsection as they rode on his horse, Bluebell. At least he finally knew her name, Naomi Hudson. What he didn't know—was how to get rid of her.

Naomi's floral scent smelled better than his horse, closer to the flower his horse was named after—Ma's favorite flower.

Ma.

Caleb sighed. Ma and Bluebell had been the only females in his life—and the one was a horse. Now, he had another woman, possibly even stronger-willed than Ma, if that were possible, to contend with. Ma wasn't going to be happy about this. She didn't like gambling and she certainly wouldn't approve of one's destiny being left to a game of chance.

Ma said if you chose right, you never have to choose again. Not that it did her much good. She chose Pa and while the two were perfect for each other, Pa didn't live to grow old with her or see any of his grandkids come into this world. But Ma was still faithful to the love they shared. No, she wasn't going to be happy—not that he intended to go through with marrying her, and of all things, tomorrow.

Marshall knew the law, he'd fix things. First thing in the morning, Caleb would ride out and talk with him.

Tomorrow was Sunday. That meant Marshall would be heading their way to go to church with them. In fact, he'd probably be at the house for breakfast and he'd certainly be there for lunch.

"Please be there before breakfast," Caleb muttered under his breath. "If not, you may be there in time for Ma to kill me."

Caleb clicked his heels against Bluebell's sides, anxious to get home. He hadn't had a chance to talk to Naomi, other than to find out her name and the fact that she would not be humiliated by a fiancée or a husband going into a saloon filled with loose women and all kinds of carousing. He needed to talk with her. Perhaps they could work something out, or maybe he could introduce her to another unwed fella. Maybe she'd take a liking to them. If he could get her to tone it down a bit, not be so headstrong, he might be able to convince another gent to take her off his hands.

When they arrived at the ranch, a soft glow illuminated the living room window. Caleb smiled. Ma left a lantern burning low for him to see when he came home. Part of him knew she did it as much for herself, so she'd know whether or not he came home at night. She could see the light shining beneath her door, and if it was dark, she'd know whether or not he'd come home and turned off the lantern.

Instead of stopping to get Naomi set up inside, he continued on to the barn. She seemed to have a penchant for being boisterous, so talking while he unsaddled the horse and stuff seemed the best option.

He helped lower her down and climbed off the horse. Thankfully, there was a full moon, so they could see faintly in the dark. "Wait here while I grab a lantern."

"You're awful quiet."

She shrugged and looked around. "I'm trying to decide why someone who apparently comes from an influential family and obviously worked hard to obtain such achievements would risk his hard-earned money gambling. Or are you risking your family's money?"

Caleb bit his lower lip to keep from coming back with an angry retort. Naomi displayed concern over Jacob gambling away provision money, perhaps her observation was merely one of concern. He didn't know her background, perhaps she grew up poor. Although, she didn't look malnourished.

"I realize that neither of us knows much about the other person, but I can assure you, I'm very responsible." Caleb lit the lantern and paused a moment, hoping she would see the confidence and sincerity in his eyes. "Whenever I choose to marry, my fiancée will have no reason to doubt my ability to provide for my family's needs."

Naomi's hands found her hips in a stance that was becoming all too familiar within the short time he'd known her. "Given you've already got a fiancée, I think you've failed to amply convince her of that."

"I'm not your fiancé and come tomorrow when Jacob sobers up, he'll be wanting to make amends with you," Caleb said. "I'm sure of it." At least, he hoped.

She turned her nose up in defiance. "I have no intention of making amends with him, so you can consider our wedding still on, and in case you are having any second thoughts, I should warn you that my daddy and two older brothers will be here for the wedding."

"And they're expecting you to marry Jacob, not me." Caleb's chest tightened. This was the first he'd heard about her family, and if she was mentioning them with a warning, it sounded like trouble. They may not take kindly to the situation. Perhaps his brother could help persuade her father into settling matters with Jacob, so they could continue with their original wedding plans—plans he didn't wish to be a part of. "I'm sure if we all sit down and talk, we can settle this. My oldest brother, Marshall, is the sheriff. He'll be more than happy to discuss the law."

"Your brother's the sheriff?"

Caleb wished he could read her expression, but the lantern flickering in the barn didn't give enough light. "Why do you want to marry me as opposed to Jacob anyway?"

She laughed, which made her appear friendlier. Naomi was also very beautiful. No wonder Jacob had swooped her up, but why was he willing to let her go?

"Giggling like a school girl isn't an answer." Caleb's patience was wearing thin and it was getting late. There were still chores to do in the morning. "Tell me why you're so bent on getting out of your engagement to Jacob."

Her smile faded. "You've seen Jacob. Isn't it obvious?"

Caleb frowned. "If it were obvious, I wouldn't be asking the question. Because honestly, I can't figure out why you agreed to marry him in the first place."

"Trust me, marrying Jacob Sinclair was not my idea."

"Your father's?"

~ 111 ~

Naomi nodded, confirming his suspicion. "Are you almost done yet? I'd like to go to bed."

CHAPTER THREE

Caleb swatted at his face as he rolled to his side on the couch and muttered in his sleep. Little droplets trickled on his face again. He wondered if it was raining. His eyelids were too heavy to open so he shielded his face with his arm and drifted back to sleep. A sudden splash of water jolted him, bringing him upright. "What in the world?"

Blinking rapidly, his vision came into focus. Ma stood over him, holding an empty glass and smiling. "Were you too tired to make it to bed last night?"

"Not exactly." He rubbed his hands over his face, wiping the water off as he tried to wake himself up, so he'd be coherent enough to break the news to Ma. His mind was clouded in a sleepy haze. "It's complicated."

Ma laughed. "How complicated can it be?"

"Good morning," Naomi said. "I thought I heard voices."

Both Caleb and Ma turned to look at Naomi standing near the hallway. She was wearing one of Caleb's shirts instead of the pale green dress she had on the night before. Her legs were bare. Caleb's cheeks warmed, and he reluctantly forced himself to turn his head. He swallowed hard, struggling to remove the image from his mind. His mind flashed to when he was still in school. He'd seen Becky Sue's calves when she hiked her dress slightly to trudge into the river's edge to retrieve her hat that'd blown away. Granted, he was the one who'd taken her hat from her in the first place in an attempt to flirt.

All-in-all, it did work to his advantage because he managed to kiss Becky Sue that day.

"I think it's time you explained complicated."

Distracted, Caleb blinked and looked at Ma. "Huh?"

"Complicated." Ma nodded her head toward Naomi. "I think it's time you did some explaining."

"You must be, Ma." Naomi walked over to Ma and hugged her.

Ma stood there, mouth gaping. She looked like she didn't know what to do with her hands and wasn't sure what to do with the half-clad woman with her arms around her.

"I'm so excited to meet you." Naomi held Ma at arm's length, either oblivious to the dumbfounded stare, or ignoring her stunned look. "I can't wait for Caleb and me to be married. I'm sorry you didn't get more notice than this." Naomi laughed. "To be honest, I only found out about it last night, but nonetheless, I'm still very excited."

"Marriage?" Ma looked from her, to Caleb, then back to her. "My son asked for your hand in marriage?"

"Not exactly." Naomi looked sheepishly at Caleb and winked. "I guess you could say he won my hand in marriage."

A storm cloud settled on Ma's features, kind of the quiet before a tornado was about to hit. "I think it would be best if you went and got dressed while I talked with my son."

"Yes, ma'am." Naomi dropped her hands to her sides, nodded and went to do as instructed.

Caleb was surprised she didn't dispute anything. Maybe if she feared Ma, she wouldn't press things when Ma told her the wedding was off. "I can't marry her, Ma."

"Do you want to explain how you won her hand in marriage?"

"I was playing cards with the guys and Jacob Sinclair bet his fiancée in one of the pots I won." Caleb sighed. "I'm hoping Marshall can help me figure out a way to send her back to Jacob."

Ma frowned. "You've got to be kidding? That old crotchety geezer?"

"They were supposed to be married today." Caleb stood and stretched to get the kinks out of his cramped body. "Now she seems to think the two of us are getting married instead, so I need to head to town early and see if I can catch up with Marshall."

"Looks like I need to wear my nicest dress to church today." Ma turned to go.

"Why's that?" Caleb asked.

"Cause I can already tell you what your brother's going to say." Ma laughed, but not the kind of chuckle someone made when they thought something was funny. "Marshall is going to tell you that you should have folded the hand, but since you didn't, you knowingly proceeded, which means I need to change and you might as well get ready too, cause unless you can sweet talk that woman…" Ma motioned wildly toward the hall leading to Caleb's room. "…into mutually agreeing to cancel the wedding, you're getting married today."

"And I can assure you I have no intention of canceling our wedding." They both turned to see Naomi standing there, smiling. She looked at Ma. "Can I help get breakfast on the table?"

"I was just coming to help as well," Mary said as she came into the room.

"Do we have company this early?" Montana stopped in the living room, his hands around his wife's waist. His eyes narrowed when he looked at Caleb. "Something we should know about, little brother?"

Caleb ran a hand through his hair, wishing there were some ravine close by that he could throw himself into. "Don't we have chores to do before breakfast? If we don't get out of the way, the women might not feed us."

Montana chuckled. "I heard Jessie and Sarah stirring. He should be out any time now. Sarah on the other hand—" He shook his head. "I heard some serious heaving going on earlier. Not sure she's feeling well today."

"I hope I am not sick like that when I am with child." Mary crossed her arms on top of Montana's and held them as he drew his wife even closer.

"I'll be glad to hold your hair back for you if you are feeling ill." He kissed his wife's cheek. "And I'll look forward to our beautiful son or daughter."

Thankfully, Jessie came out of his bedroom before Montana got any mushier. Between that and everything that happened last night, he felt like he was going to suffocate. The thought of getting married, especially to a woman he didn't know, was scary enough without having to think about having babies. He was excited about being an uncle, but getting married and becoming a father? Granted, at twenty-six, he should be thinking of settling down, but twenty-four-hour notice wasn't enough!

CHAPTER FOUR

"You what?" Jessie guffawed. "That sounds like something stupid that I would do."

Caleb aimed the cow's udder in his younger brother's direction and squeezed, splattering him with a fine stream of milk. Jessie swatted at it and ducked. When he sobered, Caleb responded, "You do realize you called yourself stupid?"

Montana leaned on the wood railing of the cow's stall while he looked at Caleb and at least had the decency to pretend to be serious about the matter. "I hope Marshall can help you out." He tipped his hat back a fraction and chewed on a piece of straw. "I'd have suggested you convince her that she's really in love with her old fiancée, but let's be honest, I doubt she ever was and the fact that you come from a family that is a lot better off than Jacob..." Montana shrugged.

"Yeah." Caleb sighed. "If she'd been there to coax him or something, I'd say for sure she was only looking for a richer husband. But honestly, I don't know what's going on or why she'd want to marry either one of us."

"You clean up fairly decent, even though you're the only one of us with blond hair—kind of the odd Kincaid out of the family." Jessie grabbed the basket to go retrieve eggs. "Maybe we can convince her that you're not one of the family and won't inherit anything. That might get rid of her."

His spirits perked up. Would it work? "Do you think Ma would go for it?"

Both of his brothers laughed.

"You know Ma considers lying right up there with the ninth Commandment." Montana straightened and tossed down the piece of straw he'd been chewing. "She'd consider telling Naomi that you weren't really her son right up there with bearing false witness. You even suggest it to her..." Montana shook his head and sighed. "That'd hurt her a whole lot more than going out and gambling did."

Caleb didn't know what the big deal was about playing cards. He went out on the town—so what? Okay, granted last night wasn't normal. He'd never brought anybody home with him or ended up engaged before. And if he was honest with himself, if he hadn't been playing cards, he wouldn't have ended up bringing Naomi home last night. Why couldn't Jacob have bet a wagon or horse, something useful?

Naomi seemed to align herself with Ma, even insisting that she ride with Ma in the wagon to church. Ma said it would be good bonding time for them. If Naomi had been his girl, in the real sense of the word, this would have been a touching moment. However, given the outlandish circumstances, Caleb had wanted the time to ask Naomi some questions. Like, why did she want to marry him? Also, why in the world had she ever agreed to marry Jacob Sinclair, a man at least twice her age?

If Caleb couldn't question his own fiancée, then he might as well not follow them to church. He rode ahead on Bluebell, figuring he'd find Marshall and ask him for his help in getting him out of this mess.

Caleb spotted Marshall's horse outside Aunt Clara's Inn. Sometimes he stopped there for breakfast on Sundays if he didn't come out to their house to eat. Marshall liked having his own space, or so he claimed. Truth was, Caleb knew he was worried that someone would come looking for him one day and the family might get caught in the middle. It was also why he'd never bothered to find a wife and settle down.

He really didn't have an excuse for not settling down, other than working on their ranch was a long, hard job and he hadn't met anyone. If he'd met Naomi under different circumstances, he may have considered pursuing the redheaded spitfire a challenge worth undertaking. She had spunk, like Ma, which meant she stood a better chance of making it in Missouri. The cold winters could be harsh, and there was always work to be done. She didn't seem to mind pitching in to help make breakfast this morning either. In fact, she was the one who suggested helping.

"What are you smiling about?" Marshall's voice startled him, and he jumped.

"I didn't see you come out." Caleb hadn't realized he'd been smiling. A pair of haunting green eyes almost made him smile again.

Marshall grinned. "You've obviously got something on your mind. I've never seen you so distracted."

Caleb took his hat off a moment to run his hand through his hair and put the hat back on. He sighed. "I went out to play poker last night."

"Let me guess, you must have won big by the way you were grinning," Marshall said. "And now you're worried about having to repent when you go into church this morning and lay a wad of money in the offering?"

"That's funny." Caleb chuckled. "Think Reverend Morgan would think anything of it if I donated a woman to the church?"

"A what?" Marshall chortled.

He'd obviously caught his brother off guard because he couldn't ever remember Marshall laughing so hard.

Marshall wiped his eyes with the back of his hand. "I'm not sure I should hear any more about your night, or if, perhaps, you should be confessing to the reverend."

Caleb frowned and backhanded his brother in the arm. "You're supposed to be helping me. I need to find out how to get out of getting hitched."

His brother quickly sobered and looked at him quizzically. "What are you talking about?"

Taking a deep breath, Caleb let out a sigh. "I was playing poker and seem to have won Jacob Sinclair's mail order bride. He didn't have anything else to bet and threw her in on the last pot. I tried to protest but had no intention of folding with a full house."

"Oh, you're going to have a full house," Marshall said. "And sounds like you've at least found the wife." He nodded toward the direction of the church, where Ma and the others had just pulled up in the wagon. Jacob, along with three other men, was walking toward the wagon. "Looks like Ma's here and it looks like your fiancée may have some company. Please tell me you didn't do anything to make them want to shoot you?"

Caleb turned and looked. "No, but Jacob seemed to have second thoughts after he lost her."

The moment the other older man with Jacob grabbed for Naomi's arm to drag her out of the wagon, Caleb took off running toward them.

CHAPTER FIVE

"You're going to marry Jacob Sinclair today and that's final." Pa grabbed her arm and started to drag Naomi toward the church. When he turned, Caleb was standing, fists clenched, in front of Pa.

"I'll thank you to take your hands off of my fiancée." Caleb focused his gaze on Pa and her two older brothers.

A taller man with brown hair, a beard and mustache, came around Caleb. He bore a striking resemblance to Montana. The missing Kincaid brother, or possibly another relative. "Please take your hands off the lady and we can clear up any misunderstanding."

"Mind your own business," Pa spat. "This is a family matter."

"Given that I'm the sheriff and her future brother-in-law," Marshall said. "I reckon that makes me family and it matters."

Pa let go of her arm. Naomi rubbed the spot he'd held. "Thank you, Sheriff. I'd be more than happy to explain."

"Ha." Pa's laugh was incredulous. "I know the way you explain things," he said. "You're just like your ma. You have a way of twisting things, trying to confuse the facts." He turned his attention to the sheriff. "And the fact is, she is betrothed to Jacob and has been for a month. She came to House Springs to marry him."

"I came to House Springs to get out of marrying him." The thought of spending her life with the old geezer turned Naomi's stomach.

"How did you come about being engaged in the first place?" the sheriff asked.

"She responded to my advertisement looking for a mail order bride." Jacob's chest puffed out with pride, making Naomi want to expel breakfast on the ground, like Sarah had done, but for different reasons. "And then I even won her hand in marriage."

Naomi planted a fist firmly on both hips. "And yet I'm the one who loses because, Heaven knows, I sure don't want to marry you and I never did."

"Give me a moment, Marshall." Caleb gently grabbed Naomi's arm and nodded away from the small crowd gathered. "Let's go talk."

She obliged, if for nothing else, to get away from her family and that awful man. "I'd rather die than marry him."

"Nobody's dying." Caleb gently rubbed her forearms.

Naomi stared at him, seeing him closely for the first time. His sea green eyes held warmth. Caleb was closer to her age, and he came from a wonderful, close family—not like hers. Since her mother died four years ago, when Naomi was fourteen, her father and brothers expected her to carry the extra responsibility left by her mother's passing. Pa began burying himself in the bottle until he came slightly out of his slump when he began playing poker—too bad he wasn't any good at it.

"Did you agree to marry Jacob when you began corresponding with him?" Caleb's pointed gaze held her captive.

"No. I said I wanted to meet him before I would agree to anything." Thankfully, she'd had the sense to make that request, not that it helped in the end. "His letters indicated that he was a widower who didn't have children and that he was closer to thirty. After I met him, I told him I was sorry that I couldn't marry him because he was not as he appeared in his letters. He claimed he hadn't lied and that he felt like a thirty-year-old, which even you clearly can tell he isn't that spry."

Caleb laughed. "Sorry. No, you're right. It's been a few decades since he was that age." He rubbed his thumb gently across her cheek to wipe a stray tear. "So how did you end up engaged to him?"

"Jacob and my pa had words. He found Pa's weakness—poker." Naomi swallowed hard. Even saying the word was like swallowing cod liver oil. "Pa had a hand he was sure he couldn't lose, but didn't have any more money, so he bet me at the coaxing of Jacob." Another tear rolled down her face and Caleb wiped it away. "You have to tell them the truth, that Jacob bet me, and he lost to you. I can't marry him—I won't."

"Nobody is going to make you marry him." Caleb leaned his head closer to hers. "I promise."

She nodded, afraid to speak, lest she break down and cry in front of everyone. Caleb took her hand and led her back to the others.

"Marshall, could I have a word with you in private?" Caleb asked. The two walked away to talk.

Naomi's heart pounded in her chest. She jumped when someone grabbed her hand, then relaxed and smiled faintly at Caleb's ma.

"You're going to make this right, Naomi, and do what's expected." Pa glared at her. "Jacob has been planning on this wedding for a month now. You can't just up and leave. It would be like squelching on our arrangement."

Naomi opened her mouth to speak, but Ma squeezed her hand, and said, "It seems it was 'your' arrangement all along. Perhaps you should go live with Jacob—since you both seem to be well suited for each other."

"What's that supposed to mean?" Pa straightened. Her older brothers, Thomas and Elisha, took their stance on either side of Pa.

Jessie and Montana stepped in front of her and Ma. Montana spoke, "It means the two of you deserve each other."

Caleb and Marshall rejoined the group.

"I've heard everyone's side of this," Marshall said. "And while Jacob may have had an arrangement to marry Naomi, he made other arrangements with Caleb to get out of his previous arrangement with Naomi's father."

Naomi breathed a sigh of relief. If she heard right, Marshall was taking her side.

Pa started to protest, but Marshall cut him off. "Hear me out. Your debt to Jacob is fulfilled, and as long as Naomi and Caleb get married today, then Jacob's debt to Caleb will be fulfilled."

If it wouldn't seem inappropriate, since Marshall was the sheriff, Naomi would hug him, and Caleb for convincing his brother that she was no longer obligated to marry Jacob.

"What about a game of poker?" Pa asked. "You play either me or Jacob, and if you win, you'll have my blessing to marry my daughter."

"I already won your daughter's hand in marriage fair and square, and I don't need your blessing." Caleb's tone was curt. "Besides that, I quit gambling because my fiancée doesn't like for me to—and I understand why now."

CHAPTER SIX

"Naomi," Pa said.

Something in his voice caught Naomi's attention. She paused in her tracks and looked over her shoulder. The others were starting to make their way to the church as well, and stopped when they heard Pa.

Caleb brought his other arm around her as they turned to face her pa. Naomi felt safe with him by her side. Feeling a sense of bravado, she straightened. "What do you want, Pa?"

His gray eyes softened, like they did when he was feeling melancholy. "Can I talk to you?" He looked at Caleb, and then back to her. "Alone."

Caleb squeezed her side, pressing her closer. He obviously didn't want her to talk with her father.

She didn't want to talk with him either, but if she didn't, he might try and stop their wedding. Best to let him say his peace. "Fine, but if you're going to try and talk me into marrying Jacob, it won't work."

Pa nodded. "I just want to talk."

Naomi and Pa walked less than ten feet away from Caleb. She dared not go farther than that, because Caleb took a step closer in their direction, indicating he wasn't about to let her get too far from him. His clenched fist and taut jaw revealed the restraint he maintained with great effort. It made Naomi smile.

"I know you got eyes for this boy," Pa said. "But I'm concerned about your future, and how well he can provide for you. Jacob said he had room for all of us on his ranch and we could be together as a family."

"Pa, we haven't been together much as a family since Ma died." Naomi sighed. "You and the boys just wanted me to look after you, and that's the same reason you wanted to move here. So, I could look after you all and Jacob, too." Naomi crossed her arms, rubbing her upper arms. She wasn't cold, but it felt like the life was draining out of her. "I can't do it Pa—I won't."

"So, you think this youngin' can take care of you?" Pa said. "Is that it?"

"Jacob lied to you about how great his place is, Pa. It's a shack, and there's another worn down shack on the property. That's where he was planning on you, Thomas and Elisha staying."

"Why that—"

"Pa," Naomi cut him off before he could use any foul language. "Stay here and let me speak with Caleb a moment."

Relief flooded Caleb's face when she began walking towards him. He headed towards her and closed the gap. "Are you okay?"

She nodded. "I know I don't have any right to ask you this, but they are family and I think my pa's main concern is where he and my brothers are going to live. Jacob promised them that they could stay on his property, but he really only had a shack, and since I'm not marrying him, thanks to you, they have nowhere to go."

Caleb's eyes widened. He looked at her pa, then her brothers, and back at her. "You want them to live with us?"

"No." Naomi almost laughed at his reaction, even though it wasn't funny. She felt guilty enough for not wanting her own family living with them. "Your family has a lot of property and I was hoping maybe they could put a shanty up on it—far from us."

"Like how far?" It was the first time she'd seen Caleb smile. His green eyes twinkled, and a set of fairly straight, white teeth showed below his mustache. She had to admit, he really was very handsome.

Naomi swallowed hard, thinking of what it would be like to kiss him. His mustache would probably tickle—or scratch her. Either way, she had a feeling she'd like kissing Caleb.

He said something, and she jumped. "Huh?"

"How far?"

She giggled nervously. "Far enough away that they won't be expecting me to wait on them hand and foot."

"Does that mean you don't want to wait on me hand and foot either?" Caleb's left eyebrow arched.

"I didn't say that." Her cheeks warmed. "I would gladly take care of my husband." Naomi mentally added, *as long as it wasn't Jacob Sinclair.*

Caleb tilted her chin up with his index finger and stared into her eyes. "Good.

He took her hand and led her back over to her father. Caleb extended his hand for Pa to shake.

Pa looked at it hesitant, before slowly reaching out and shaking Caleb's hand.

"My name's Caleb Kincaid." He released her pa's hand. "I thought it best for us to properly meet before I marry your daughter."

"I'm Eli Hudson," Pa said. "You can call me Eli."

"Will do." While Caleb may have been younger, barely older than either of her brothers, he was more mature—sure of himself. Naomi couldn't have found a better husband for herself if she'd gotten to do her own choosing. "Your daughter tells me you and your sons are in need of a place to stay. So, if you find it agreeable, you and the boys can stay in the bunkhouse and work on the ranch in exchange for food and a roof over your head."

"You want us to work for you?" Pa frowned.

Caleb nodded. "Everyone on our ranch pulls their own weight—nothing wrong with an honest day's work."

Pa nodded toward Caleb's family. "What about them? You don't have to ask your folks?"

"No," Caleb said. "My family will do what is right and they won't see someone go without a place to stay as long as the person is willing to help themselves."

"Right kind of your family."

Naomi had to agree with her pa. The world needed more Kincaids. She only hoped she could live up to the family's standards.

"How about we head into church since it's about to start?" Caleb smiled and squeezed her hand. "I hear there's supposed to be a wedding after church today."

CHAPTER SEVEN

Caleb was relieved that Jacob didn't stay and attend church. Although, he needed to be in church—just not today. The last thing he needed was a big commotion going on in church. He had enough to repent for, he didn't want to add shooting a man to the list. Not that Jacob would get violent or try to forcibly take Naomi away. Caleb wanted today to be like any other ordinary Sunday at their quiet little church. Given everything his brothers had gone through, a nice, quiet and uneventful day was in order.

As it was, being a Kincaid, where mishaps seemed to follow, Caleb held his breath all through the wedding ceremony, afraid Naomi's pa or brothers might have a change of heart. To his relief, they sat quiet as tumbleweed on their pew. They'd even taken a moment to swipe some of the dust from their clothing before entering the church—showed they had some respect. Caleb didn't know much about his soon-to-be in-laws, so observation was his only means of assessing them.

After the church service, when Reverend Morgan presided over the wedding ceremony and pronounced them husband and wife, Caleb was so excited, he hugged Naomi. He took a step back. His cheeks warmed. While it may have been okay to touch his wife, he didn't want to press her to be affectionate. He felt guilty, even though it wasn't his fault, that she ended up being forced to marry. She should have had the choice to marry for love. Hopefully one day, they would grow to love each other.

His family was the first to come congratulate them, followed by hers. After all the well wishes, Caleb put his arm around Naomi and announced, "My wife and I will be staying in town tonight and will be home tomorrow."

Naomi's eyes narrowed. "Where are we going to stay?"

"I thought it would be nice to stay at Aunt Clara's Inn," Caleb said. "She makes a great apple pie."

"That she does. I can almost smell it—just thinking about it." Marshall laid a hand on his stomach. "In fact, I could go for a piece right now."

Caleb jabbed him in the side with his elbow. "I'm sure Ma has something back at home that you could eat. Don't you, Ma?" He raised his eyebrows toward Ma and quirked his head toward Marshall.

Ma laughed. "Why don't you join us for lunch, Marshall? You can help get Naomi's family set up down at the bunkhouse."

Dawning resonated on Marshall's face and he chuckled. "You know, come to think of it, I'm really in the mood for pie."

"Good." Caleb pushed him toward the door of the church. "Why don't we get out of here?"

They stepped outside. The sun was so bright, Caleb raised his arm to reposition his hat when a shot rang out.

The next thing he knew, everything was moving in slow motion as Marshall drew his pistol and fired repeatedly. Each ping of the weapon echoed in Caleb's ears.

Naomi screamed.

Was she hurt? Caleb looked at her. She still wore the light green dress she was wearing when they met—he'd have to see to it she got something new to wear, even though the dress brought out the deeper shades of green in her eyes. Naomi had a hand over her mouth. There wasn't any blood. She wasn't hurt. He staggered backwards. Someone caught him. The voice—it was familiar.

"We need a doctor—somebody go get Doc."

Caleb nodded and closed his eyes.

CHAPTER EIGHT

"I got the bullet out of his shoulder, but he's lost a lot of blood." Doc stretched his back. Silvery strands of hair mixed heavily with black ones. Weariness etched his features. "I'd like to keep him here, so I can observe him overnight."

"I'm staying, too." Naomi walked over to where Caleb was lying on a wooden table and took his hand.

"No," Caleb muttered. "You go home and get some rest."

"I'm not going anywhere, Caleb Kincaid." Her tone was crisper than she'd intended. "I intend to spend my wedding night with my husband, no matter where that is."

He laughed and winced in pain. "There's that fiery redhead I met in the saloon."

"If you weren't already shot, I'd…" Naomi pulled her hand from his and planted a fist firmly on each hip. She hated saloons and hated gambling even more. Even if it did land her with a more appealing husband than the one Pa was going to make her marry. She still had no intention of condoning such talk. It made her appear gaudy.

"Kiss me?" Caleb winked at her.

Doc chuckled. "Don't mind him, he's taking laudanum. He may not act like himself for a bit, but it will help with the pain."

"It still does not excuse my husband's behavior." Naomi tilted her nose in the air. "And he'd best keep in mind that I have no intention of dragging him out of a saloon again."

"So, you will let me stay next time?" Caleb raised his head a fraction and it fell back down against the table with a thud. "Ouch."

"Serves you right." She couldn't resist making a faint smile but moved closer to his side and laid a hand on his arm. "Now, mind your manners and rest. We need to get you to build your strength back up."

"I'll stay with you." Marshall startled her.

"That's not necessary." There was so much commotion today. All Naomi wanted to do was rest. Her emotions wreaked havoc within her—yet she willed herself to stay strong for her husband's sake. "Caleb needs to rest."

"That he does," Doc said. "I think he'll be more comfortable if you boys could move him to the cot over in the corner."

Marshall and Montana gathered on either side of the table and swooped Caleb off the table. He moaned. "I'm not a sack of potatoes. Be careful."

Naomi started toward the cot, only to see Caleb's ma was already turning back the covers. "Set him down here gently." Ma patted the spot and moved out of the way. "Naomi, will you find us some fresh rags that we can use to clean him up a bit?"

She was thankful to have something useful to do. Naomi did as she was instructed and brought a bowl with fresh water over. She set it on the table next to the cot and wrung out one of the rags.

Caleb's shirt had already been removed. She hadn't paid much attention until now, when she noticed his lean, muscular build. The fact that his muscles were evident meant he was accustomed to hard work. It was

~ 135 ~

encouraging to know that prior to their meeting, he didn't have a habit of being idle. No doubt, he would also have a better chance of recovering. That wasn't something Naomi cared to think about. Sitting on the edge of the bed, she wiped at the offensive red smear across his chest. "Did you find out who did this, Marshall?"

He looked down and then away. Naomi wondered if he'd heard her question. Then Marshall nodded and swallowed hard—she could see the little knob in his throat move. Finally, he looked at her. His eyes held great sadness. "He was shot because of me."

"You didn't do nothing to get your brother shot." Ma grimaced.

"A while back, I jailed Levi Tucker on account he murdered a man." Marshall took a deep breath and exhaled slowly. "His brother, Colt, didn't take it well when his brother was lynched. Best I can gather, he finally decided to come after me for bringing Levi in."

"So, it wasn't Jacob?" Naomi felt like a great weight had been lifted off her shoulders. The thought that Caleb may have been shot because of her had been eating at her gut from the moment it happened. She hadn't paid attention to the man lying on the ground, or all the excitement because she could only focus on the bloodstained shirt on her new husband. She ushered up a short prayer, vowing to do all she could do to care for her husband, and anything else God wanted, as long as he didn't take Caleb away.

CHAPTER NINE

As Naomi sat on the edge of the cot next to Caleb, she dipped the rag in cool, fresh water from the basin her brother-in-law had filled for her. She wrung out the rag and laid it back across Caleb's forehead. She wiped her hands against her dress to dry them. "I'm worried about him, Marshall. His fever still hasn't come down."

Marshall laid a reassuring hand on her shoulder and gave it a gentle squeeze. "His body is trying to fight against any infection."

Naomi nodded. She knew he was right, but it didn't keep her from being concerned.

"At least he has stopped moaning, so the pain medicine Doc had you give him must be working."

"Marshall?" Caleb stirred. He tried to raise his arm, letting out a few foul words with the effort that made Naomi's eyes widen and her cheeks warm.

"I'm here, Caleb." Naomi moved to let Marshall take the spot near his brother.

She could see the effort it took Caleb effort to moisten his lips and swallow. Naomi went to the cabinet across the room and poured water from the pitcher into a glass. She returned and handed it to Marshall, who helped Caleb hold his head up while he held the glass to his mouth for him to take a sip. Naomi took the glass back from Marshall and returned it to the top of the cabinet.

"You know," Caleb said, his voice barely a whisper. "I didn't even want to get married today." Caleb reached for Marshall with his good arm, but his fingers slid down the sleeve of Marshall's shirt and his hand landed on his own stomach. He drifted back to sleep.

Naomi turned and walked back over to the cabinet. She didn't want Marshall to see her face. Right now, she wanted to cry. She'd been so absorbed with her own feelings through everything—how her own father could gamble her away, like she meant nothing. Then Jacob did the same thing. She hadn't bothered to consider Caleb's feelings. He only wanted to go out for a night on the town—not end up forced into marriage the next day.

Being the kind and considerate man that he was, Caleb agreed to marry her so that she wouldn't be forced into marriage with Jacob. That was a big sacrifice to make. While all she could think of was herself.

"He didn't mean that."

She jumped, startled by the nearness of Caleb's brother. "Yes, he did." Naomi turned to face Marshall. "Caleb is a good man. He was willing to put his own freedom aside to marry me, a woman he didn't even know, just to save me from having to spend my life with a man I didn't want to be with."

"I know my brother." Marshall tilted her chin up to face him. "He wouldn't have married you if a part of him didn't want to."

"Well, it's obvious his decision is weighing heavily on his mind if he is thinking about it in his condition." Naomi looked over at her husband. "I've been selfish not to consider his feelings in all of this, and as soon as he's well enough to fend for himself, I plan to have our marriage annulled." She turned her attention back to Marshall. "Since you're a lawman, promise me you'll help."

"I can't…"

"We both want what's best for Caleb." Naomi clutched his forearm in her hands. "Promise."

Strain marred Marshall's otherwise handsome features. He closed his eyes and nodded. "If it's what Caleb wants."

CHAPTER TEN

Caleb's fever broke around sunup, so the doctor let them take him home a couple hours later, when it seemed evident that it wouldn't return. The doctor gave Naomi instructions for what to do if his fever returned and told her to send someone for him. Otherwise, he would be out to their house in a couple days to check on Caleb's progress.

Caleb was still in too much pain and heavily medicated to notice how quiet Naomi was, but his ma noticed, no doubt because of the quiet ride home from the doctor's. After they'd gotten Caleb settled in his bed, and Ma ran everyone else off so that he could get his rest, she cornered Naomi in the kitchen. "You gonna tell me what's up with you and Marshall?"

Naomi's mouth gaped. She busied herself with making something for Caleb to eat. The doctor said that getting Caleb to eat would help him gain his strength and the laudanum would not bother his stomach as much.

Ma came over to her, put her arm around her waist, and gently turned Naomi's face up so she could see her. "You don't look guilty," Ma said. "Sad." She nodded. "You definitely look sad."

A tear rolled down Naomi's cheek.

"Hmm. I guessed right, didn't I?"

When Naomi nodded, it was as if she'd shaken loose whatever was holding back the waterfall of tears that streamed down her face.

"It's all right." Ma wrapped her arms around Naomi and gently rubbed her back. "This whole ordeal has been an emotional train wreck for all of us."

"It's not right." Naomi sniffed between sobs.

"I know, dear." Ma continued to comfort her, not realizing Naomi hadn't finished saying what she was feeling.

Naomi lifted her head from Ma's shoulder and composed herself, wiping the tears from her eyes. She shook her head and looked in Ma's eyes. "Caleb shouldn't have had to marry me against his will. He's too good of a man and deserves better."

Ma laughed. "Too good a man?"

Naomi nodded.

"He is a good man—all my sons are. But if you ask me, he couldn't have picked a better woman on his own." Ma hugged her again. "You stayed by my son's side and cared for him all night, never leaving his side. Marshall told me how much you fretted over him. Your concern was genuine—not something someone did begrudgingly because it was expected. You showed true love, and that love between the two of you is only going to continue to grow."

"But..." Naomi sobbed. "He didn't want to marry me, he said so himself."

"Of course, I wanted to marry you." Ma and Naomi turned at the sound of Caleb's voice. He braced himself against the back of a chair, slightly hunched over.

"You're too weak to be up and about." Naomi quickly closed the gap between them. She stood on his good side and put her arm around his waist. He placed his uninjured arm around her. "Let's get you back to your room."

"There's my spitfire," Caleb whispered into her ear as they walked.

"Behave yourself, Mr. Kincaid." A flicker of encouragement danced within her chest. She reminded herself not to get her hopes up. "The medicine you are taking is not letting you think clearly."

Naomi helped him sit down on the bed. He drew her down with him, causing her to land next to him.

"I'm thinking plenty clearly—certainly enough to know I don't like to hear the sound of my wife crying." He pulled her closer and leaned his forehead against hers. "Now, tell me, what makes you think I didn't want to marry you, and was that why you were crying?"

"You asked for Marshall last night, and then you told him you didn't want to marry me." She sniffed, trying to keep from breaking down in tears again.

"Aw, sweetheart." Caleb kissed her on the top of her head. "I didn't want to marry you at first because we didn't get a chance to know each other properly." He brushed a couple of strands of hair out of her face and caressed her cheek, rubbing it gently with his thumb. "You caught my attention from the moment I first saw you, and to be honest, the thought of you marrying Jacob or any other man didn't set well with me."

"Really?" Naomi searched his face, afraid to believe her own ears.

Caleb nodded. "Really. You're the woman I want to spend my life with."

Naomi threw her arms around his neck and kissed him.

He winced in pain.

"I'm sorry. I should have been gentler."

"I'll show you gentle." Caleb drew her close and kissed her tenderly, igniting a fire.

"You don't know how much I want you." She blushed at her own admission. "When you're ready, and we can really be together as husband and wife."

Caleb smiled and kissed her. "I'm more than happy to oblige."

"Just promise me one thing," Naomi said between breaths while he continued to plant kisses along her neck.

"What's that?" His voice was husky.

"Promise me that 'until death do us part' is a long time off 'cause I need you—here with me."

"I promise I'll never willingly leave your side," Caleb said. "Because it is right where I belong."

Mail Order Brides:
Marshall's Bride

By Susette Williams

CHAPTER ONE

House Springs, Missouri —later in July of 1843

Lizzie McCleary stepped down from the stagecoach, aided by the driver as he held her hand. "Thank you."

A stained, toothy grin appeared as he tipped his hat to her in response. "Obliged to help, ma'am. I'll have your baggage ready in a moment."

With that, he climbed back up on top of the stagecoach and loosened the leather straps securing her and the other two passengers' luggage. He tossed them down to the other stagecoach hand who had come back out of the depot.

"Good luck, dear." Virginia, the elderly woman, and her husband, that she'd ridden with on the stagecoach from Virginia were an adorable couple. Virginia hugged her. "I hope you and that young fella will be as happy together as me and Richard have been for the last forty years."

"Don't you mean forty-three, dear?" Richard said, correcting his wife.

She laughed and gently patted his arm. "They weren't all happy years, my dear." Virginia winked at Lizzie. "All marriages have their ups and downs, but if you both work together, it will all work out."

Lizzie nodded politely and thanked the woman. It was easier than saying she couldn't care less, she wasn't marrying for happiness this time. Choosing to become a mail order bride was not a decision she made easily—it was made out of desperation. The money her husband, Jeremiah, had left her upon his death was almost depleted. Had she not skipped a meal a day, it would have already been gone—like Jeremiah. Some days the loneliness overwhelmed her so much, she wished the ground would open up and swallow her. Then at least she could be with Jeremiah again. "Why did you leave me?"

"I'm sorry, dear. Did you say something?" Virginia looked at her quizzically.

"No." Lizzie shook her head. "I was just mumbling to myself."

"I can tell you're nervous about meeting your young man." Virginia smiled knowingly, yet Lizzie knew the woman had no idea of the turmoil running through her. "Make sure to inquire in the depot or the mercantile, and I am sure someone can help you to locate your law-man. No doubt he's on duty, keeping the town safe." She smiled. "My daughter, Cecilia, said the law men in this town do a wonderful job and upholding the law."

"That is good to know. Thank you, again." Wanting to end their conversation before Virginia got carried away again, Lizzie walked toward their luggage and retrieved her floral valise along with the leather trunk that had belonged to her husband. She couldn't bring herself to part with his few belongings. Sometimes, at night, she pulled out one of his shirts and inhaled the fragrance, laying her head against the fabric, just to feel close to him again. Her favorite smell was when Jeremiah smelled woodsy from a fire burning—oak or pine. Lizzie instinctively inhaled deep to no avail, her memories of the scene long-since faded. She didn't have any clothes that smelled like her husband in winter since it was summer.

The thought of never smelling that scent again saddened her.

Coming to America was supposed to be an exciting adventure for them. Instead, it turned out to be a nightmare for her, one she desperately wished she could wake up from. It was Jeremiah's dream to make a way in the new country, a land of prosperity, as he called it. Since he didn't live long enough to even stand on this country's soil, Lizzie planned to fulfill their dream, and one day, when she got to Heaven, they could exchange stories about the adventures they both had encountered during their time apart.

Lizzie spotted the sign for the jail. Taking a deep breath, she squared her shoulders and headed across the street. She was a survivor—a strong woman, as her husband had told her on numerous occasions. He'd also told her she was stubborn. Today, she had to agree. She was too stubborn to give up. No matter how much she detested the thought of marrying another man, she'd do it, and she'd be the best helpmate that she could be for him in exchange for him providing for her needs.

The bell above the door rang when she entered. A lean man with blond hair looked up. He didn't fit the description of the man who had placed the ad for a mail order wife.

"Excuse me." She moistened her lips. Slightly embarrassed, she swallowed hard, trying to rummage the strength to continue. "Do you know where I might find the marshal?"

He chuckled. "Sure you don't mean Marshall? Lots of people get his name confused, especially since he's the sheriff."

"Oh." She blinked, looked away, and then back at him. "He always signed his letters with an extra 'l' I thought perhaps it was just a misspelling." Her cheeks warmed. "He said he was a law-man. I assumed that was his position."

"That's all right, ma'am." He smiled and stood, coming around his desk to greet her. "Why don't you set your luggage down and have a seat."

She set them against the wall, near the door, so that they would be out of the way.

He pulled up a chair for her to sit, facing his desk, then he went back and took a seat. "I'm Deputy Chase. Perhaps I can help you since Marshall is out of town right now."

Lizzie sat down, feeling as if her heart had plummeted with her body. "When will he be back?"

Deputy Chase shrugged. "Don't know. Could be a couple weeks."

"What?" Had she heard him right? "Where am I supposed to stay in the meantime?"

"You could always stay at the inn," Deputy Chase said. "You look a bit flushed. Are you sure I can't help you? Perhaps if you told me what the problem is?"

"He's my fiancé." Her voice sounded flat and lifeless, much like she felt inside. Marshall was her last hope.

"He's your what?" Deputy Chase blinked several times, leaning his forearms against his desk. "You must be confused."

"We're supposed to get married." Lizzie pulled out the stack of letters from her drawstring purse. "He sent me these letters. I was hoping to stay at his place upon my arrival."

"May I?" Deputy Chase reached across the desk and took the correspondence from her. He opened up a couple of the letters, shaking his head as he read. "I don't know what to say."

CHAPTER TWO

Lizzie sat in a wooden rocker, looking around the living area of Marshall's mother's home. It was a lovely home and much larger than she was accustomed to seeing, especially in this country. There were only a few feminine touches, like the curtains. The living room, kitchen and seating area for meal time was cozy. Undoubtedly the family gathered together often by the looks of the slightly worn leather on a couple of the chairs. The property had been a bit overwhelming to see, as Deputy Chase had pointed out the expanse when he brought her to the home.

Ma, as she'd been instructed to call her, had sent her daughter-in-laws to prepare a snack for them. She sensed the woman wanted to talk in private. Lizzie was thankful the woman merely needed to see the stack of letters to be convinced that Lizzie was who she claimed to be. "I must say, I'm quite surprised your son never mentioned me to any of his family, not even to the deputy he works with."

Ma's laugh sounded a bit shaky. Lizzie wondered if she still had her reservations—not that she could blame her. She doubted any of his family would fully trust her until Marshall returned and cleared up the matter.

The other three women joined them with refreshments, setting the tray of lemonade and fresh baked bread on the table in front of the couch. Lizzie's stomach grumbled. She placed a hand against it, even though it wouldn't do any good toward quieting it. Her cheeks warmed. "I'm sorry. It's been a while since I've eaten."

"Here, let me get you something." The woman with brown hair quickly sliced a piece of bread and put it on a small plate before handing it to Lizzie, along with a glass of lemonade.

"Thank you... I'm sorry, I don't remember your name."

"Mary." She smiled. "I'm married to Montana. Naomi and Caleb were just married nearly two weeks ago." She nodded toward the blonde who was with child. "And Sarah is married to Jessie."

"I have to admit," Sarah said, rubbing her protruding belly. "I never figured Marshall for the marrying type, especially after what happened to Caleb."

Lizzie glanced at Naomi. "What happened to Caleb?"

Naomi looked hesitantly at Ma and then back at Lizzie. "The brother of one of the men Marshall arrested, who was later hanged, came after him, but he shot Caleb by mistake."

"Oh, my. I hope he is okay." A wave of nausea came over Lizzie. She felt queasy. Did she really want to risk becoming a widow again so soon? And what if Marshall got killed before they married? Where would she go?

"He's doing better." Naomi frowned. "But I wish he would take it easy. He is supposed to be supervising Sarah's brothers while they work on fixing some of the fencing in the south pasture." She sighed. "But if I know him, he won't be able to resist the temptation to get in there and show them how it's done."

"How long has Marshall been gone?" Lizzie asked. "Deputy Chase mentioned Marshall has a place closer to town. Perhaps I could stay there so as not to intrude on your family." It would also give her time to think.

"Nonsense," Ma said, taking one of the glasses of lemonade from the tray. "You're practically family and it is no intrusion at all."

"Thank you." Lizzie thought it best to be polite. After all, she was a stranger in their home and they hadn't expected her arrival. She took a sip of her lemonade and sat it down on the table, then began to tear off tiny pieces of her bread and eat them. Her stomach was still uneasy, but hopefully, the bread would help to settle it some.

CHAPTER THREE

One week later

"Yahoo! Marshall, you old coon hound, you." Deputy Chase chuckled, got out of his chair and came around and hugged Marshall, patting his back briskly.

Marshall didn't know what to do. Normally, he didn't hug other men, especially his deputy. He cleared his throat. "Perhaps you'd care to explain?"

Chase blushed and regained his composure. "Sorry, boss. I was just excited for you."

He was amused, to say the least. He'd gone to St. Louis because he'd heard Levi's other brother, Trevor, lived there. After having Levi Tucker lynched and shooting Colt because he tried to avenge his brother's death, and inadvertently shot Caleb, Marshall wanted to make sure that Trevor didn't have a vendetta against him as well. If Trevor did, he hid it well because he was one of the most peaceful men that Marshall had ever met. Trevor said he'd parted with his brothers a long time ago because of their wild side. He was the only one of the three who settled down and took a wife, who recently had a baby. Once Marshall felt reassured that Trevor meant him and his family no harm, he'd headed home—to what, he wasn't sure. "You were excited because I came back in one piece and not full of bullet holes?"

Removing his hat, Chase ran a hand through his unruly blond hair and laughed as he put his hat back on his head. His lopsided grin made Marshall smile. "You don't have to keep the secret any more, Marshall. In fact, Lizzie's here."

"Lizzie?"

The deputy nodded. "Your fiancée, Lizzie."

It was Marshall's turn to laugh. "Don't you think if I had gotten engaged I'd know about it?"

His deputy stared at him, no traces of humor evident.

His jaw dropped.

"You were serious?"

Chase nodded slowly.

"And this woman, you said her name is Lizzie?"

He nodded again.

"She's here?" Marshall asked. "And she told you that she was my fiancée?"

This time, when Chase nodded, Marshall got irritated. What were they playing, a game? Chase reminded him of one of those wooden puppets with strings attached that a theater guy had brought through town last year. His head bobbled peculiarly, as if someone else were manning the strings to operate him—just like the puppets. "How about you just tell me what in tarnation is going on, so we can stop playing this guessing game?"

After Chase relayed what little information he knew, Marshall was still confused. He'd never written a mail order bride—or anybody else for that matter. Why did this woman think she was his fiancée? Could one of his adversaries have coerced her to gain his trust as some part of an elaborate plan? There was only one way to find out.

By the time he arrived at Ma's, his mind had played out half-a-dozen scenarios and reasons why this strange woman would show up on his family's doorstep. Either she had to be connected to one of his adversaries, or she was delusional. Whatever the case, he would either arrest her or send her packing. His family had already had enough to deal with this year, they didn't need another threat.

Marshall tied his horse up to the post out front and went inside. A beautiful brunette was sitting on the couch, folding laundry. When she saw him, she stopped, clutching the undergarment to her chest, she stared at him. Their gaze continued to remain locked, until a noise in the kitchen distracted him and he looked up past her.

"You're home." Ma dusted the flour from her hands onto her apron, then removed the apron and set it on the back of a kitchen chair before joining them in the living area. "This is, Lizzie. Lizzie, meet my oldest son, Marshall." Ma's smile was a bit shaky. No doubt she'd been trying to make the best of things since the stranger arrived. He'd make it up to her later, and he'd chastise his brothers for letting down their guard. They should have dealt with this situation the moment it arose. Maybe moving out hadn't been his best decision. If anything, he'd thought his family would be safer, but trouble had a way of finding a person if it was looking hard enough.

Lizzie sat the garment down and stood. She moved closer to Marshall and extended a hand. "It's a pleasure to finally meet you."

The first thing he noted was her Irish accent. He took the hand she offered but didn't release it immediately. Her hand was not as soft and delicate as she looked. She'd apparently known hard work. Lizzie's hair was worn up, but a couple of curly strands had worked their way loose. Eyes the color of emeralds stared into the depths of his soul. His breath caught. Whoever was playing tricks on him had chosen the appropriate bait. She was beautiful enough to throw any man off guard. Her face was expressionless. When he let go of her hand, she clasped both of hers together in front of her. "Please, have a seat. Then you can tell me what you're doing here."

Ma took a seat as well. Since Lizzie didn't appear to pose any immediate threat to his family, it was safe to question her here. Understandably, Ma would want to know about the woman she had put up for the past week—he didn't think it right to exclude her from the interrogation.

Marshall sat back in the chair and crossed his leg, his right ankle on top of his left thigh. Wiping at some dust, he realized how worn his boots were getting. Time to order a new pair. Perhaps Ma would take care of that for him, or he could have his fiancée. He resisted the urge to laugh as he looked at her. She wasn't his fiancée and he didn't have any business entertaining such thoughts. His life was a dangerous one—possibly from the likes of someone like her. "Why don't we start with, you tell me a bit about yourself."

"You've read my letters." She shrugged. "They pretty well sum it up."

"Let's pretend I haven't read your letters, because quite honestly, I haven't."

Lizzie opened her mouth as if to say something, and then closed it. She stared at him, like he wasn't even there, her eyes glassy.

He hated to press her in her apparently fragile state. He'd seen shows before, when he'd visited St. Louis, and he hated to admit it, if she was acting—she could put them all to shame. Marshall would be the first to commend her on her performance. "Please, let's start over so that we can get to the bottom of all of this. Why don't you tell me about yourself?"

"I was married." Lizzie looked down at her hands in her lap. Her thumb strummed gently across her wedding ring finger, where a white line was evident, but no ring. "My husband, Jeremiah, and I were the best of friends growing up. It seemed only natural that we should marry." She expelled a deep breath. "He wanted to see the world and begged me to come with him to America for an adventure. Jeremiah said he had plans laid out for us when we arrived, but what those plans were, I really don't know." She wiped at a tear. "He said his mouth hurt one night when we were going to sleep. There was a bump above one of his teeth and he was planning to find someone on the ship who could take a look at it, but the next morning, he wouldn't wake up."

"He died?" Marshall asked.

Lizzie shook her head. "No, not right away. He ran a fever and remained unconscious. Two days later, he stopped breathing and was buried at sea." She sniffed. "All I have left are my memories and a few of his belongings that I haven't been able to part with."

"That's understandable," Ma said, and took a seat next to Lizzie, clasping her hands around the other woman's. "I still have a few things that belonged to my husband, too."

"You do?" Lizzie looked at Ma. That bit of knowledge apparently offered her comfort.

"I'm sorry for your loss, ma'am, but I still don't understand how you come to think that I'm your fiancé."

CHAPTER FOUR

"I thought it was so sweet how you told your mother that you were the man of the house since your father died, and that she didn't need to worry, you would take care of her."

Marshall stared at Lizzie as she talked. How did she know these things? There's no way he was writing her in his sleep, but there was no other explanation—or was there. His head slowly pivoted toward Ma. That was the conversation he had with her, so nobody else would know about it unless one of them had said something about it—and he sure didn't.

"Do you still have these letters?" He bit his tongue and avoided adding, *that I supposedly sent you?*

Lizzie's eyes widened slightly, then slanted. "Yes."

"May I see them?"

She nodded and rose from her seat. "Just a moment. I'll get them."

As soon as she was out of the room, Mary, who'd been eavesdropping from the kitchen area, bustled toward them. She stared at Marshall, a frown marring her otherwise pleasant features. "You didn't send for Lizzie, did you?"

Marshall would have laughed if it weren't so frustrating. Instead, he shook his head. "No, but I fully intend to get to the bottom of this."

"Ma, do you mind if I talk to you alone for a minute?" Without waiting for her to answer, he stood and headed for her bedroom. He noted the look of hesitation on her face. No doubt he'd shared that same expression when he was a young boy and about to get a paddling for getting in trouble. Both Pa and Ma had made it a point of taking them aside to discipline them and helping them to understand what they had done wrong to earn their spanking. Perhaps he should ask Ma what her punishment should be—if she was guilty. But why would she have done it in the first place?

He nearly bumped into Lizzie in the hall. She had the letters clutched close to her chest. She reminded him of an innocent fawn, staring blankly. Her eyes were mesmerizing. A man could get lost in them, but he wouldn't. No matter the reason for her being there, his job was dangerous. "I'm not sure how things got mixed up." Marshall cleared his throat, so it wouldn't sound so husky. "But given that my job as sheriff is a dangerous one, I can't marry you."

"My previous husband didn't have a dangerous job, and yet he's dead," Lizzie's tone was flat. "No one is guaranteed tomorrow, Mr. Kincaid. The reality is, you need someone to look after you, and I. . . I'm a woman on my own, with no real means of providing for myself. Which means either I marry again, or I end up working in a saloon, which is an idea I find distasteful to say the least. At least, you are an upright, law-abiding citizen, a man I can trust."

While she may have had time to reason things out, he'd only found out he had a supposed fiancée earlier that day. He still needed time to think this through.

She must have sensed his hesitancy. Lizzie handed him the letters. "Please take time to consider things, because whatever you decide directly affects my future."

Marshall nodded and passed her. As he paced the foot of Ma's bed, while she took her good ole' time coming into the room, Marshall tossed his cowboy hat on the bed and ran his fingers through his hair. Now he understood why Ma used to say she wanted to pull her hair out. She must have felt helpless, dealing with a frustrating situation—like he did right now.

As soon as Ma walked in the room, he blurted out, "You did it, didn't you?"

"Did what?" Ma tried to look innocent by pasting on one of her naïve expressions.

His laugh sounded incredulous to his own ears. He wasn't amused by her game. "You know, when Deputy Chase congratulated me on getting engaged, my first thought was someone from my past was trying to get close to me, possibly to kill me." He grunted and began pacing. If the letters in his hands had been someone's neck—it would have snapped. "I never would have suspected that my own mother would turn against me."

When he turned, he saw sadness in her eyes. "I didn't turn against you."

Expelling a deep breath, he walked over and stopped in front of Ma. "Then why would you write a total stranger and tell her I would marry her without even talking to me about it?"

Ma looked down. She reminded him of a small child that knew they'd done wrong. But how could he be angry at her? He loved her.

"I'm not going to be around forever," Ma said. "Someone's gotta look after you, keep you company when you get old."

"I'll be fine."

"It ain't good for a man to be alone. You need someone special in your life, and when I saw how happy Jessie was, I wanted you to be happy, too," Ma said. "So, I wrote in response to a mail-order bride ad."

Letting out a frustrated sigh, Marshall shook his head. "Ma, marriage ain't like one of those catalogues at the general store. You don't just look at the pictures and point out what you like. You and Pa got to know each other, and you both fell in love."

"If you give it time, you'll fall in love, too." Ma laid a hand on his forearm. "She needs you Marshall. Just promise me you'll read her letters and think about things before you miss out on the opportunity to marry a really wonderful woman." Ma smiled and removed her hand, then walked over to her dresser and opened a drawer. She pulled out a stack of letters and came back to stand in front of him again. "I got to know her first in her letters, and then even better as we've cooked and cleaned and talked in person. Here."

He took the letters Ma handed him. At least now he'd be able to know what she'd replied to the letters she thought he'd sent her.

"I'm not always going to be around to look out for you, Marshall." Ma reached up and kissed his cheek. "Give her a chance. Promise me you'll at least read her letters."

Marshall nodded as he stared at the letters in his hands. He'd do that much. After losing Pa, he didn't want to think about losing Ma. She wasn't that old, but there were enough things, and even bad winters, that had claimed the lives of several people he knew.

"And Marshall."

He glanced back at Ma.

"I'm pretty sure she's pregnant. Somebody's got to take care of her—she won't make it on her own."

CHAPTER FIVE

Ma had sent her sons' wives out to work in the barn, so she could speak with Lizzie alone. Marshall was still in Ma's bedroom. Knots tightened in Lizzie's stomach as she fretted over what the other woman might have to say. Was Marshall sending her away? If he didn't write her those letters, then who did? Was this all some sort of cruel humor? Concern-etched creases marred Ma's face. Lizzie wrung her hands together in her lap. She should have never agreed to come to America. Nothing had gone right from the moment she and Jeremiah had set sail.

Sitting down next to her on the couch, Ma gently laid a hand on top of Lizzie's and sighed. "I don't know how to tell you this."

"He doesn't want to marry me, does he?" She knew it, her fear finally verbalized. Lizzie closed her eyes, her head hung low. Any final glimmers of hope vanquished. "It doesn't matter. He's probably wiser not to marry me since it seems everything associated with me dies—my husband, my dreams…"

"You have a lot to live for."

Lizzie's head shot up at the sound of Marshall's voice. He stood less than ten feet away from her, clutching their letters.

"My mother said she believed you are with child. Are you?"

"What?" How could she be? She wasn't married—anymore. Jeremiah died over two months ago. Lizzie thought about her womanly time. She hadn't really paid attention and thought her grief had just overwhelmed her body. Instinctively, she moved one of her hands from Ma's and touched her stomach. "I. . . I don't know."

"You haven't been feeling well and especially when we've been preparing meals." Ma smiled. "I was like that when I carried the boys, and Sarah did the same thing for a few months, she was always getting sick."

"I never dreamed. . ." A tear trickled down her face. Her lips curled into a smile. "I'll always have a part of Jeremiah with me."

"Ma, do you mind going and checking on Sarah and the others while Lizzie and I talk?"

"We'll go visit Doc later." Ma hugged her.

Lizzie nodded, still overwhelmed by the idea that a baby might be growing inside her stomach. A baby—hers and Jeremiah's. Her gaze darted to Marshall. She hadn't noticed that Ma had gotten up and headed out the door.

"Do you mind if I have a seat?"

She shook her head. "No, please, sit down."

Marshall sat in the rocker, near the end of the couch, where she was sitting. He crossed his ankle over his thigh, still holding their letters within his large hands. She noted earlier that he was taller than his brothers that she'd met over the past week. Between his added height and being the only brother to have both a mustache and beard, he appeared more daunting. Yet his greenish-brown eyes held warmth, which made her feel safe and comforted.

"I've had a chance to read through the letters." His thumb stroked the stack of letters in his hands that he was referring to. "And I guess you've figured out by now that I didn't write them, my mother did."

Her eyes widened. She laid a hand against her chest, not that it would steady her rapidly beating heart. "But. . . Why would your mother write them?"

"She's worried that she'll die one day and that I'll be left alone." He smiled, shook his head and expelled a slow, steady breath. "Ma knows I'll always look out for her, and with my job as sheriff, I've been afraid to get married. Especially after Caleb got shot."

"You can't put off the inevitable," Lizzie said. "If something is going to happen—it's going to happen. I no more could have stopped my husband from dying, even if we'd never gotten on that ship to come to this country. Only God can control whether or not we die or live another day."

"That's a lot of wisdom from someone who has lost so much."

Lizzie smiled for the second time in months. "I think the hardest thing about losing Jeremiah was losing my friend, and now..." She lowered her hand to her belly. "I may always have a part of him with me."

"If you don't mind my asking, how long did you and Jeremiah know each other before you were married?"

Warmth flooded Lizzie as she talked freely about her feelings and her relationship with Jeremiah. "We were friends since we were five or six years old, when we started school together. As we got older, he would walk me home and we'd stop to explore along the way. Then we'd help each other get chores done so we could go play some more."

"I had a friend like you when I was young."

"What happened?"

"She caught sickness, around when my pa did, and neither one of them made it." Marshall stared down at the letters, but Lizzie doubted he was really seeing them. No doubt his mind wandered back to the girl he'd lost. Just like Lizzie's mind had conjured memories from her past.

"I'm sorry for your loss."

Marshall nodded and gazed at her. "I doubt I can be half the man that Jeremiah was, but if you are still interested in being my wife, I can promise that I will look after you and your child, but I will want children of my own someday as well."

"I understand. It wouldn't be fair to deny you your own children, but I do want this child..." She looked down at her stomach, and back at Marshall. "If I am with child, to know about his father, because I can't pretend that Jeremiah never existed."

"I understand." Marshall uncrossed his leg. "What do you say to going into town to see Doc and then to see the preacher about getting married?"

"I'd say I'm a bit nervous."

Marshall chuckled. "So am I."

CHAPTER SIX

Marshall paced the waiting area of the doctor's office like an expectant father. How long would it take Doc to examine Lizzie? Waiting alone was nerve-wracking. He didn't know whether to curse Ma, or kiss her, for getting him into this predicament. At least she and the girls were kind enough take Lizzie's belongings to his place and tidy up, or as Ma put it, *add a feminine touch*. Ma thought things should be special for their wedding night.

He chuckled to himself.

After being away for a couple of weeks, he'd only wanted to come home to his own bed. The last thing he ever expected was to be getting married and taking a woman back home with him. Thoughts of waking up next to her made his heart race. Lizzie was a beautiful woman, and from her letters, along with speaking to her for what little he had already, he could tell she was caring. Any man would be lucky to have her as his wife. The only question was, would she be happy enough with another man?

While Grace had been the love of his life, he'd had eleven years to overcome the pain of losing her. Many nights he'd laid in bed and thought about what their lives would have been like had she lived. No one knew that he had intended to ask her pa for her hand in marriage. Once his pa got sick, Marshall had gotten busy, picking up the extra slack from Pa being down under the weather, as they'd called it at the time. Then, when their lives were upended like a tornado had run smack-dab through them when Pa died, Grace got sick as well. He never should have allowed her around to help when Pa was sick, but he'd wanted his parents to see what a wonderful woman she was before he announced his intent to make her his wife.

Both he and Lizzie knew pain. They weren't walking into marriage with high expectations. Love and respect were things that would grow over time. For now, they shared a common bond—one of having known love and loss. In time, he would expect her loyalty and affections for him to grow.

His sense of confidence wavered as he thought of the little life, possibly growing inside Lizzie. A baby might make her attachment to her first husband's memory grow stronger. It might be the backwards way to do things, but he'd court Lizzie after they were married. That way, he'd have the opportunity to win her heart, and he'd make sure to be a real father to the baby. He'd had enough experience at that over the years, helping to raise his younger brothers.

The door opened, causing Marshall to jump. Four long strides closed the gap between him and the doctor. Doc would have made a good poker player, because his expressions were hard to read. "Well?"

A corner of his mouth quirked upwards. "I've seen many anxious father's before, one being your brother, Jessie, but nonetheless, I will let the missus tell you."

"She's not the missus, yet." Marshall lowered his voice, "and if you don't mind, I'd rather you not tell anyone about her condition, or how far along she is. We need time to talk about things and decide how much we want to let others know. I presume Lizzie told you that she's a widow?"

Doc nodded. "Yes, and I recommend that Lizzie not overdo things because she has already been through enough stress."

Marshall agreed.

"I have to say," Doc said, "your daddy would be mighty proud of the man you have become. Lizzie told me that you both have plans to wed when you leave here, even though you knew she might be with child from her husband."

He shrugged. Marshall hadn't thought of how his pa would have felt. Obviously, he had Ma's blessing since, she more or less arranged the marriage.

The doctor was still speaking. Marshall forced himself to focus on what he was saying. "If you weren't marrying Lizzie…" Doc shook his head. "I hate to think of what would become of her and the baby. They're mighty lucky to have you."

"Thank you." Marshall shook Doc's hand.

"And don't think I didn't notice how you weaseled information about Lizzie out of me." He chuckled, crooking his neck in Lizzie's direction. "Now, go get your lady."

Marshall smiled and went to Lizzie, helping her off the table. A memory flashed through his mind. Less than a month ago, Caleb had laid on this same table—bleeding from a gunshot wound.

"What's wrong?" Lizzie asked. "You look pale. Are you feeling sick?" She reached up and placed the back of her fingers against his forehead.

He took her hand in his and stared into her eyes. "You know my job is dangerous?"

She nodded. "We already discussed that."

Glancing at the table, his eyes narrowed when he looked back at her. "My brother laid on that same table only a few weeks ago, shot by a man that was trying to kill me. I don't want to put you or the baby in danger."

Lizzie smiled unexpectedly and reached up to gently stroke his cheek. "You always worry about everybody else, don't you? And that is something I admire about you, Marshall. But without you, well, I don't want to think about what would happen without you. I need you, and you need to stop worrying. I know we can make this work together, and we will face whatever comes our way."

Touched by the warmth of her words, Marshall leaned forward and kissed Lizzie. She startled slightly, and smiled, so he continued, deepening the kiss until he thought his heart would explode.

When their kiss ended, her cheeks were flushed. Her smile lit up her eyes. "I've never kissed anyone with a beard and mustache before. Jeremiah always had a clean-shaven face."

"Good," Marshall said. "Then you won't be likely to forget who you're kissing."

Her cheeks turned rosier. "Don't worry, I won't forget."

CHAPTER SEVEN

A tear trickled down Lizzie's cheek as she gazed at the beautiful pink and cream roses Ma handed her for her wedding.

"They're nothing fancy," Ma said. "Just some from my rose bushes."

Lizzie hugged Ma. "They're beautiful. I can't thank you enough for your kindness."

"I know you'll take good care of my boy." Ma wiped the tear from her cheek. "And he'll take care of you and that youngin'."

She nodded. "I know he will."

While she and her husband had a long-time friendship before marriage, she and Marshall would have the experience of getting to know each other. She used to enjoy meeting new people and finding out about their lives, but the long journey and some of her experiences in this country had dampened that adventure. Coming to House Springs, and meeting Marshall's family stirred a hope that had almost vanquished—life didn't look so bleak anymore. Lizzie owed his family more than her gratitude for their unconditional love.

As she walked to the altar to meet Marshall, she couldn't help but feel a bubble of excitement and joy. Having his family all attend their wedding was wonderful. She almost wished that her parents and her younger sister could have come, but travel was beyond their means. It had taken Jeremiah a couple years to save up for their voyage here, along with provisions he had hoped to acquire. At least her family had attended her and Jeremiah's wedding. When she got the opportunity, she would write them and give them all the news that had transpired since she'd left Ireland. At least now, she'd have some good news to share.

It was hard for Lizzie to concentrate on every word that Pastor Morgan said. Having been a few months since she'd been with a man, her body was acutely aware of Marshall's presence, especially after he'd kissed her earlier.

When the preacher pronounced them man and wife, Marshall's brothers whooped and hollered when he kissed her. She, on the other hand, savored the warmth of Marshall's body pressed closely to hers as a surge of emotion coursed through her beneath his kiss, promising her of more to come.

His whiskers tickled as he nuzzled up close to her ear and whispered, "I love the way you blush when I kiss you."

Lizzie shook her head and smiled. "What am I going to do with you?"

"I can think of a few things." Marshall winked. "But that'll have to wait until later." In a louder voice, Marshall announced, "Why don't we all head over to Aunt Clara's for dinner. My treat."

"I'm in," Jessie said.

"I've never been one to turn down free food." Montana patted Marshall on the back and then hugged him. "Congratulations, big brother. Same to you, ma'am." He tipped his hat to Lizzie.

"Call me, Lizzie, please."

"Welcome to the family, Lizzie." Montana hugged her, which quickly turned into everyone hugging and congratulating them.

Marshall kept an arm around her waist as they walked to the restaurant. In the midst of everyone, she felt a little overwhelmed, yet surrounded by such love. She hoped they would have a large family one day, if it meant having such closeness. Her family was quieter, especially since her only sibling was a sister, two years younger than herself. She'd miss being around the whole family when she went to her new home with Marshall. This past week with his family had been pleasant. Lizzie looked forward to getting to know the whole family better. "You could have invited your aunt to our wedding."

"What aunt?"

"Aunt Clara," Lizzie said. "I feel bad having lunch at her place and she wasn't even invited."

The sound of Marshall's deep laughter made her smile. "She's not my aunt, just a woman in town who has an inn and serves some of the best food around—outside of Ma's cooking."

"Well, let's hope my name gets added to the list of women whose cooking you enjoy." Lizzie smiled up at her husband.

He squeezed her closer and kissed the top of her head. "I'm sure it will, but it's going to take a lot of meals for me to be persuaded."

"Ha." Lizzie smirked. "If you can't decide within a week, then we'll both be eating at Aunt Clara's or your mother's every day. That, or you may end up taking residency at either location."

Marshall stopped and pulled her gently to face him. Tilting her chin up with his index finger, he leaned his forehead against hers. "I'm sorry, Lizzie. I was only teasing."

"I know, so was I." Lizzie laid a hand on either side of his waist and raised up on her tiptoes to give him a brief kiss. "And I promise to never send you packing." She released him and turned to follow the others. "However, if you don't like my cooking, I may have to move back home with your mother so that she can give me lessons."

He chuckled. "You're not going anywhere without me."

CHAPTER EIGHT

Marshall's arm casually draped behind the back of Lizzie's chair. He took joy in the simple pleasure of watching his new bride eat the rest of her apple pie. Aunt Clara had insisted that she bring dessert for the newly married couple and he'd never been accused of turning down dessert. His wife had struggled to finish all of the roast, potatoes and carrots they had for dinner. She didn't appear to have as big of an appetite as their sisters-in-law. That would change, with time. Lizzie wouldn't have to worry about where her next meal was coming from. It bothered him that she'd ever had to be concerned about anything. Thankfully, her worries were behind her because he was there and would take care of her and the baby.

A smile formed on his face when he saw Deputy Chase walk into the restaurant. His friend could honestly congratulate him this time, since he was married.

"Excuse me," Marshall whispered in Lizzie's ear. "I'll be right back."

She nodded and smiled at him, then turned her attention back to Montana, who was relating a story of their youth. During their meal, his brothers had told enough stories about Marshall and gotten most anything they could have considered embarrassing out of their system. If they hoped to deter Lizzie, it was too late—she was already his wife. His grin grew wider.

As Marshall closed the gap between him and Deputy Chase, he realized his friend wasn't smiling. So much for hoping for an uneventful wedding. Silently, he prayed nothing had gone wrong, and that no other criminals, or their family, had come looking to pick a fight with him. "What's up, Chase?"

"Sorry to interrupt your family gathering." Chase glanced at the other Kincaids and back. "You really got married today?"

Smiling, Marshall nodded. "Yep. Sorry we didn't have a chance to invite you. It was kind of sudden."

"I'll say." Chase chuckled. His expression sobered. "Anyhow, some stranger showed up asking for Lizzie McCreary. I was pretty sure it was your Lizzie."

Marshall straightened. "What's he want?"

"I don't know. He wouldn't say. Says he'll only talk with Lizzie or Jeremiah." The deep breath Chase expelled, reached Marshall's face. They were obviously standing too close, and in this summer heat, it was hard to miss any breeze, no matter how small. "I don't know, Marshall. If you ask me, I don't trust the guy."

"Did he say what his name was?"

"The guy has red hair, hard to miss, said his name was Samuel O'Brien."

"Where's he now?" Marshall glanced at his wife. When she looked at him, he forced a smile and nodded before turning his attention back to his deputy.

"He's waiting outside."

"You go on outside and keep an eye on him." Marshall clasped Chase on the shoulder, taking a step toward the door with him. "I'll talk to Lizzie and see if she's heard of the guy or not. Then at least maybe I'll have an idea of his intentions. I'll be out in a couple minutes."

"Sounds like a plan." Chase tipped his hat and headed out the door.

Walking over to his wife, Marshall knelt down beside her and took her free hand in his. If she flinched when he mentioned the man, it will tell him all he needed to know. "There's a man outside, claiming to be Samuel O'Brien. He says he'll only speak with you, but if you don't know him, I have no intention of letting him talk to you directly."

Lizzie's brow creased. "Samuel O'Brien?"

"It's okay if you don't know him." As Marshall stood, he paused to kiss his wife on the temple. "I'll be back in a little while." He averted his gaze toward Montana and motioned with a slight nod toward Lizzie. "Keep an eye on my wife." Montana's smile faded. Thankfully, Montana had picked up Marshall's undertone.

He hated to admit it, but he was glad Lizzie didn't know the man, because he really didn't want her talking to him. Especially if Chase had doubts about the man. Give him ten minutes alone with the guy and he'd talk. Marshall would make sure of it.

CHAPTER NINE

One look at Samuel O'Brien, and Marshall understood Chase's mistrust for the man. He stood around the same height as Chase, just under six feet, but that's where any similarities veered. Samuel had reddish-orange hair with a matching gruff beard and mustache. His clothing looked like he'd rolled around in the dust and made ill attempts to swipe away the dirt from his clothing. The man didn't look to be the sort of person with whom Lizzie would willingly associate. Whatever he wanted with his wife, he'd make sure he found out. Trouble had visited his family's doorstep enough lately—it was time to meet it head on and squash anything before it had a chance to cultivate.

"My deputy tells me you've been asking about a woman?"

"Yeah, you know where I could find Lizzie and her husband, Jeremiah McCreary?" The man had an Irish accent, less pronounced than Lizzie's.

"Where do you know them from?" He decided to wait to reveal any information until he learned what the man's intentions were. If he'd known Lizzie or her husband well, seemed he'd know of her husband's death, especially if he had managed to follow her to House Springs.

"Jeremiah is my kin, my uncle's son." Samuel's squared shoulders, clenched fists and glare was a sign he was looking for trouble.

"I take it you weren't close?" Marshall couldn't prove whether or not the man was who he claimed, but if Lizzie didn't know him, he wasn't around enough for her to remember him. Lizzie said she and Jeremiah had been childhood friends, and then sweethearts, yet the name did nothing for her memory. "Seems Lizzie would know you if you were related."

Samuel gave him a dirty look. "I don't like the way you say her name, and if you let me talk to her, you'll see she does know me."

Marshall straightened. He didn't much care for this man's attitude, and it wasn't helping Samuel's cause by being rude. "When was the last time you saw her?"

"I don't see what business it is of yours, Sheriff." Samuel's tone was clipped. "Given I haven't done anything to break any laws."

"That I know of…" Marshall let his words trail off. "Truth is, your cousin never made it to America. He took ill on the ship and was buried at sea."

"What?" The color drained from Samuel's face, making his pale skin even paler. "That can't be." He staggered a couple steps, visibly shaken, and clasped onto the wooden hitching post. "What about Lizzie and their belongings?"

"Their belongings?" Deputy Chase asked.

Marshall's eyebrow arched. He'd caught that part, too. "What are you looking for, Samuel?"

The front door to Aunt Clara's opened and Lizzie came out.

Marshall's heart plummeted in his chest. She didn't need to be here right now, especially in her condition. He took a few steps toward her, but she'd already headed down the stairs and met him at the bottom.

"I'm sorry, it took me a bit to remember Samuel's name." She glanced toward the man. "Jeremiah always called you, Carrot Top, and I'd plumb forgotten your real name. It's been, what, seven years since we've seen you?" She looked at Marshall. "I mean, since Jeremiah and I last saw you."

"Is it true?" Samuel asked. "Was Jeremiah buried at sea?"

Lizzie nodded. "I'm afraid so. He complained of a toothache for a couple days and then took fever and passed away a few days later." Her head lowered. "He never got to fulfill his dream of coming to America."

"What happened to his belongings?" Samuel looked at her anxiously and approached.

Turning to face Samuel, Marshall positioned himself between the man and Lizzie. "That's a mighty peculiar question to ask?"

"Jeremiah was in possession of some papers of mine." Samuel's hands had balled into fists again. "He intended to meet me in North Carolina once you both arrived."

"I'm sorry." Lizzie placed a hand against Marshall's arm. "Jeremiah told me he had a surprise, but that's all. I wish I had even known where to look for you. I did write his family and told them the news."

"You're sure nothing was with his belongings?" Samuel glared at Marshall. "Or are you holding out on me?"

"I'm sorry." Lizzie moved her hand from his arm to her chest. "I'm afraid I honestly have no idea of what you're talking about. If Jeremiah was holding anything for you, it is news to me. He only had a small trunk with some clothing and his Bible. The only reason I've even held onto it was to keep a part of him close to me, but now…"

"Now what?"

Deputy Chase gripped Samuel's arm when he took a step closer toward Marshall and Lizzie. "Allow the lady to speak. She's clearly been through enough."

"Or did she and the sheriff find out about our gold claim and get rid of my cousin?"

"Gold claim?" Lizzie asked. "What gold claim?"

"The one we purchased together in North Carolina," Samuel said. "And don't think I'm going to let you cheat me out of it."

"I'll be happy to look through Jeremiah's things, but honestly, it may very well have been buried at sea if he had it on him because I didn't even know about the claim."

"Hmm." Samuel clearly didn't believe Lizzie.

What Marshall knew of her thus far, and felt in his heart, was that she was not an evil person. If anything, his mother was the dishonest one, but her intentions were good, and God judged a person's heart. "Why don't you spend the night in town, and tomorrow Lizzie will go through Jeremiah's things to see if she can find the papers in question? If she can't, you'll have to go and fill out paperwork to see if they can issue you new papers. I'm sure if you explain the circumstances and no one else lays claim, you shouldn't have a problem."

"I don't see there is much that I can do, but I expect you to meet me here tomorrow at noon."

CHAPTER TEN

Marshall stood in the doorway of their bedroom, staring at his wife. No sooner than they arrived back at his place, Lizzie insisted on looking through Jeremiah's things. Not something any man wanted on his wedding night—to have his wife handling her dead husband's clothing, conjuring up memories from their past. Her life was with him now. Or was it? If she had known about the claim, she would have never placed an ad to be a mail order bride, and they would have never met. Her only purpose of finding a husband was to have someone to look out for her.

"It's not here." Lizzie had even checked the lining to see if there were any loose seams. She sat on the bed, Jeremiah's Bible in her hands, rubbing her fingers across the engraved title. "I haven't even read the Bible since we took off on our voyage. But Jeremiah wouldn't let it out of his sight, kept it close to his heart and would quote scripture. He was always proud that he could remember scriptures without having to look them up."

Not knowing what to do, Marshall continued to lean against the doorway. His wife was beautiful, and he wanted to kiss her, be with her—not have an invisible wall that he couldn't compete with. Apparently, being noble didn't equate with things working out for the good guy. Lizzie deserved whatever was best for her and her unborn child.

A scripture verse came to mind, *"Finally, brethren, whatsoever things are true, whatsoever things are honest, whatsoever things are just, whatsoever things are pure, whatsoever things are lovely, whatsoever things are of good report; if there be any virtue, and if there be any praise, think on these things."* Marshall had thought on these things, which was why it was hard to not think of his wife. She reflected all that was good.

Lizzie opened the Bible. She blinked rapidly, looked at Marshall and then back down again. Her mouth opened a fraction and closed.

He moved closer. "What's wrong?"

"His Bible." She pulled a piece of folded paper out and laid the Bible on the bed.

Marshall noticed a good chunk of the pages in the Bible had been hollowed out. Undoubtedly to give Jeremiah a place to hide the papers in question. It would have been genius, in Marshall's opinion, if he'd destroyed a different book, something other than God's holy word. "May I look at the claim?"

Lizzie handed him the paper. Marshall sat on the bed next to her and unfolded the paper. "Everything looks in order."

She nodded.

"What would you like to do?"

She looked at him hesitant.

Marshall tensed. She didn't want to tell him. "It's all right. Whatever you want to do, I'll stand by your decision."

"I'd like to go back to town and clear this up today if you don't mind."

"If that's what you want," Marshall said, "then that's what we'll do."

He handed back the paper to her, which she folded and placed in the Bible before packing it in the trunk with

Jeremiah's clothing. Marshall carried the trunk out for her and put it in the wagon. Lifting her, he placed her on the seat.

"Thank you."

It was hard to trust his voice. A nod was the only response he could give. They rode in silence, each consumed with their own thoughts. Marshall's thoughts were more his worst fears—that she was thinking of leaving him. He felt like he was headed to a funeral. The only problem was, he was the one dying inside. How could one woman come to mean so much to a man so quickly? Her letters. They had let him see a glimpse of her heart that she'd poured out on every page. Earlier that day, he'd felt excited at the prospect of getting to know everything there was to know about each other as they shared the rest of their days together. Who knew that would end the very day they were married? Marshall prayed that God would intervene and not leave him to such a cruel fate—again.

Samuel had gotten a room over the saloon. Marshall instructed Lizzie to wait outside while he went to get him. He didn't have to go far, because Samuel was seated at the bar, nursing a shot of whiskey.

He gulped down the rest of his drink when he saw Marshall and climbed off the bar stool. "You have something for me?"

Marshall realized this time he was the one clenching his fist instead of Samuel. "Lizzie asked me to bring her back to see you."

"That's my girl. I knew she'd do the right thing."

The right thing, in Marshall's opinion, would have been to run Samuel out of town, but he was her kin, by marriage. Marshall followed him out to the wagon and then helped Lizzie down.

She walked to the back of the wagon. "Would you mind?"

Swallowing the lump in his throat, he grabbed the trunk from the back of the wagon. "Where would you like for me to put it?"

"Just give it to Samuel."

"Did you find something in Jeremiah's stuff?" Samuel's eyes widened, like a child at the merchant store, who was about to get a special treat.

"Just open the Bible and you'll find what you're looking for."

Samuel knelt on the wooden platform in front of the saloon. He quickly opened the trunk and rummaged through the clothing until he found the Bible. The way he grabbed the cover of the book, turned it upside down and shook to release any loose paper, showed the man clearly had a lack of respect for the Bible. All he sought was greed.

When Samuel saw the paper, he tossed the Bible down and grabbed the paper, quickly opening it to examine its contents. He shouted for joy, stood and grabbed Lizzie, swinging her around.

"Stop!" Marshall demanded.

To Marshall's relief, Samuel lowered Lizzie back to her feet. She took a step back.

"Come with me, Lizzie." Samuel grinned wide. "We can live out the dream, make a go of it together."

"I'm married."

"What?" Samuel squinted. "Not any more. Jeremiah is dead. You said so yourself."

"Marshall and I were married today. My life is here, with him." She hugged Samuel. "This was your dream and Jeremiah's. It was never mine."

"I don't understand."

Marshall wasn't sure who was more bewildered, him, or Samuel.

"The claim is yours, and just yours," Lizzie said. "Go on and fulfill your dream, make a life for yourself. I truly wish you the best."

Samuel folded up the claim and put it in the pocket of his trousers. He put the contents of the trunk back and went to hand it to Marshall, but Lizzie reached out. "Keep it. Perhaps you can use Jeremiah's clothes. They're not doing anybody any good sitting inside the trunk."

"Thank you, Lizzie."

After Samuel went back inside the saloon, Lizzie turned to Marshall. "We're going to have to work on your communication."

"My what?"

"Your family has gone on and on about how you always have something to say, yet you didn't say a word the whole way here."

"What was I supposed to say?"

Lizzie shrugged. "Maybe how you felt?"

Marshall laughed. "I wasn't sure how you felt, and I wanted you to be free to do whatever you wanted."

She nodded thoughtfully. "And what if I left with Samuel?"

"If that's what you wanted to do, I couldn't stop you."

"And you would have been okay with my leaving?"

He swallowed hard and looked away.

Lizzie reached up and turned his face back to hers. "Good, ol' Marshall, who always looks out for everyone else, but himself. What do you want?"

"I want you." Her green eyes pulled him closer, calling him to explore her very soul.

"I want you, too," she whispered as their lips met.

He'd longed to kiss her since earlier. It was something he would never get enough of. When their breaths steadied, he stroked the side of her face with the back of his fingers. "Why did you stay?"

"The Bible says, *'but lay up for yourselves treasures in heaven, where neither moth nor rust doth corrupt, and where thieves do not break through nor steal. For where your treasure is, there will your heart be also'* and I knew that gold would not bring me happiness."

She lightly kissed his lips.

"Jeremiah was my friend. I'd known him most of my life, and yet I didn't know that his reason for coming to this country was to pursue fortunes." Lizzie sighed. "I thought he wanted an adventure, a chance to charter new territory and create a place for us and our family. But in reality, he'd only buried the desires of his heart. The whole way back into town, I knew what I desired, and that was you."

Marshall wanted to shout louder than Samuel had, instead, he smiled. Then he remembered something he'd wondered about. "Why didn't you tell Samuel about the baby?"

"When I set off for America, I told my family goodbye because I knew I would likely never see them again," Lizzie said. "And while Samuel was family by marriage, I'm married to you now. I want my child—our child, to look up to you and the good examples that you and your brothers are, so that all of our children grow up to be just as wonderful as you and the rest of your family are and I look forward to spending the rest of my life with you."

"I think it is time that we go home and begin our new life together."

"I'd like that."

Marshall hoisted Lizzie up into his arms and kissed her before setting her on the wagon seat. There was one thing he was certain of, he would treasure her always.

Mail Order Brides: Husband of the Bride

By Susette Williams

CHAPTER ONE

House Springs, Missouri —December of 1843

"Apple pie, Ma?" Strands of Naomi's red hair brushed against Ma's arm as she peeked around her shoulder. "You already have stew cooking and I'm pretty sure both of these are favorites of Doc. Any chance you're trying to get him to stay around for dinner?"

Ma patted Naomi's hand as she reached for some crumbs that dropped on the table. "Mind your own business and help me get these pies into the oven."

Naomi chuckled and grabbed a pie. She followed Ma to the oven, opened it and put the pie in, then she moved aside for Ma to slide her two pies in as well. "Just seems like an awful lot of pie."

"Hmph." Ma put the pies into the oven, closing the door with a little more force than she intended, causing it to make a loud thump. "If the man is going to come all the way out here and check on the girls, he might as well be fed a good meal for all his trouble."

"Given the way I've seen him looking at you—it's no trouble."

"I've half a mind to wipe that smile off of your face." Ma couldn't help her curt tone. It irritated her that Naomi was reading things into the situation. "I would hope that all you girls learn the importance of being neighborly."

"Is there a neighbor coming by?" Mary asked as she walked into the room, touching a hand to her brown hair in its tidy bun—always the perfectionist, prim and proper.

Ma hid the smile that threatened to come, content to let her daughter-in-law remain bewildered. Her sons had all married very different women. Mary never let anyone see the less than perfect side of her, even after she lost the child she was carrying two months earlier. If she was feeling any pain, she continued to keep her feelings to herself. Naomi on the other hand, seemed to be outspoken enough for the both of them.

Her family was growing since Lizzie was due to have her baby in January, and Sarah's baby would be there in the next three or four weeks, possibly in time for Christmas.

A knock sounded at the door.

"I will get it." Ma frowned at her daughters-in-law. "The last thing I need is the two of you getting all school-giddy on me and carrying on like you were delirious with a fever."

Mary's eyes widened, and her mouth dropped. Granted the poor woman had no idea what Ma was referencing, but Ma had no intention of giving Naomi a chance to spread idle gossip either. Otherwise, Mary was sure to join in with the banter.

When Ma opened the door, Doc tipped his hat. "Good afternoon, Ma. I'm here to check on Sarah. How's she doing today?"

"She's fine," Ma said. "Think she is getting a mite bit nervous about the baby coming." Ma stepped aside. "Won't you come in?"

He did as instructed. Putting his medical bag on a table, he took off his coat and hat and hung them on the coat rack.

Doc walked further into the room. "I see your other daughters, at least two of them, are also doing well."

"For now." Ma narrowed her gaze toward them. When Doc looked at her, she quickly smiled. She started down the hall. "Shall we head back to Sarah's room?"

Chuckling, Doc followed her. "I take it your daughters-in-law are trying your patience?"

"Something like that." Ma stopped outside Sarah's door and knocked. She waited for a response before entering.

Sarah was sitting in a wooden rocker, crocheting a blanket for the baby. Hopefully she would have it finished in time. Ma didn't have the ability to help Sarah because she didn't know how to crochet, although Naomi had tried to teach her when she helped Sarah and the other girls learn. It had been enough for her to learn to use the sewing machine that the boys had bought her for her birthday a couple years ago—her fingers weren't accustomed to doing dainty stuff with fancy needles and looping yarn.

"Doc's here to see how you and the baby are doing." Ma moved aside for him to enter Sarah and Jessie's room. "I'm going to go out and see what is taking Lizzie so long. She went out to get a blanket she left in the wagon." Ma turned to address Doc. "Marshall and Lizzie are going to be staying here for a bit, seeing how there's been a lot of flooding with all the rain we've been having."

He nodded. "I haven't been able to get out to the Jenkins in a week. Hoping he didn't die of pneumonia."

Touching his arm reassuringly, Ma offered what comfort she could. "You know his missus will take care of him, and I sent Sarah's brothers over to cut plenty of firewood for them. She'll keep him warm and well taken care of."

"I hope you're right, Ma." Doc sighed. "You go on and check on your daughter. Perhaps when I'm finished, I could trouble you for a cup of hot tea?"

"I've got a nice pot of stew on too, thought you might be hungry."

"You know me well." Doc winked at Ma.

Her heart skipped a beat. Feeling it flutter in her chest concerned her—not enough to trouble Doc with though. She wiped her hands on her apron, leaving the bedroom door open on her way out.

She paused in the kitchen long enough to ask Naomi and Mary if Lizzie had returned. Confirming she hadn't, Ma asked them to set the table and keep an eye on dinner while she went out to the barn. Grabbing her red shawl off a hook near the back door, Ma bundled it around her shoulders. A fine mist of rain filled the air, forcing her to duck her head and shield her face in the cool breeze that pelted her skin with cold moisture. The cloudy sky made it appear later than it was, given sunset was still a ways off, even if the sun had chosen to hide.

At least it wasn't snowing, not that it wasn't much comfort to Ma, given Marshall and her other sons had set out to see if they could help others in the territory who were trapped or endangered by flooding. Thankfully, her daughters-in-law were all safe—which was one less thing to worry about.

Ma stepped carefully around a mud puddle to open the barn door. She needed to put some straw down over it before anyone walked through it and tracked dirt into the house.

There weren't any lanterns lit in the barn. Given how gloomy it was, she thought her daughter-in-law would have brought one outside with her. Of course, Ma hadn't either. She reckoned neither of them had much sense. "Lizzie, you in here?"

"Ma."

She faintly heard her name before a loud moan. Her heart raced faster than a team of wild horses as she rushed toward the groans coming from the far end of the barn. "Where are you, Lizzie?"

CHAPTER TWO

Ma didn't even breathe heavy as she helped Doc carry Lizzie into Marshall's old bedroom and get her situated on the bed. The woman had an endless mountain of strength. Didn't she tire with all the kin she had to look after, especially with two grandchildren on the way? And one of them was so anxious to meet the rest of the family, it was trying to be born a month before expected. Even that didn't appear to sway Ma—she belted out orders, taking command of the situation. She was a woman to be admired and revered.

"I'm going to ride out and see if I can't find Marshall." Ma patted Lizzie's hand.

Lizzie gripped Ma's hand in both of hers. Panic etched her face. "Don't leave me."

Bending to kiss Lizzie on the head, Ma smiled faintly. "It'll be all right child. Doc's here." Her words were tender and soothing. "He'll take care of you 'til I get back with Marshall."

Shaking her head, Lizzie's eyes began to tear up, then she winced in pain—probably from the onset of labor. "Please don't go."

Pleading eyes looked at him. Ma said, "She wants me to stay. Would you mind going and finding one of my sons to round up Marshall?"

Doc almost laughed. She wanted *him* to go? "And who's going to deliver the baby if I leave?"

"I delivered one—once." Ma looked hesitantly at Lizzie, then at her other daughters-in-law, one of which was due in a few weeks. "The others were cattle." She glanced back at Doc. No doubt she feared sending any of the women to look for help with the rain and flooding.

She was a good woman—and no doubt she would do her best, but he couldn't risk Lizzie or the baby's life. Doc sat on the bed next to Lizzie and laid a hand on her arm. "Ma's a strong woman and capable of handling herself on a horse. I think it would be safer if she rode out to find your husband instead of one of the other girls going, don't you?"

Lizzie looked at the others. A tear trickled down her cheek.

"I'll go." Naomi took a step forward. Before Ma could utter a protest, Naomi hurried from the room.

A loud moan drew their attention back to Lizzie. It didn't matter how he or the others felt—the baby was coming—today.

Doc would do whatever he could to save both of their lives. He knew from experience, he needed to focus on saving the mother first, even though all new mother instincts were to save their young'un. Having lost his own wife during childbearing, he wished there was something he could do to stall the baby's entry into the world, in case something went wrong, so Marshall could be here—in case he needed to say his goodbyes or grieve with his wife. He'd become a doctor, striving to learn all he could, so that maybe, just maybe, he could help others not have to undergo the same feelings of loss he'd endured.

By the time Doc had moved here, Ma had already been a widow. He admired how strong she was in spirit and in body, raising four boys on her own. Even after a decade here, he still didn't know her first name. He wondered if she knew his—he'd never heard her call him anything other than Doc. If he was still welcomed for dinner, he'd ask her what her real name was then, because she wasn't his ma, she was a vibrant, older woman—one he wanted to share more dinners with on a regular basis. He was tired of eating alone.

Preoccupied with his thoughts, and checking on Lizzie's progress, Doc hadn't realized Ma had sent the other women out to retrieve clean towels and water. At the moment, he had enough concern of his own. "The baby's breech."

Ma stared at him. There wasn't much that silenced her, except fear.

He winked at her, hoping to offer some reassurance. "I'm going to need your help, but we can do this."

She nodded, visibly shaken if the blank stare and her eyes widening was any indication. "What do you need me to do?" she mumbled.

"For starters, tell me your first name." Doc smiled, hoping to relax her. "I can't keep calling you Ma. After all, you're not my mother."

Lips pursed, it appeared she wasn't going to tell him anything. Her frown eased. "Jenny. Now surely, you've got something more than talking that we should be doing, because it ain't going to get this baby born."

Doc smiled. "No, no it isn't." He cocked his head toward Lizzie. It wasn't hot in the room, but beads of sweat formed on her face as she bit her lower lip and squeezed a handful of the cover. Undoubtedly gripping Jenny's hand with force as well.

Jenny's jaw twitched.

"Keeping our voices down and remaining calm will help the new ma." He nodded toward Lizzie.

Jenny looked at her daughter-in-law, let out a slow, calming breath and began praying out loud. When she finished, she asked Doc what to do next.

He was glad she'd thought of praying, something he often did after-the-fact, not as soon as he really needed to because he was accustomed to reacting to situations and taking charge of things quickly—like now.

"If you can help keep Lizzie calm and keep her fighting the urge to push that baby out, I'm going to have to try turning the baby around in there. If not, it may come into the world feet first." He didn't want to mention the complications that could arise from that happening.

CHAPTER THREE

Marshall shot through the bedroom door like the house was on fire. His eyes lit up once he was inside the room, and he looked like he wanted to turn around and run back out the door. He was as white as snow, not the clean new fallen flakes, but his skin was getting there.

"Do you want to help clamp your son's cord?" Doc asked, holding the baby up. He turned him to face Marshall, the cord was still connected to his mother.

"What?" he stammered. Between Marshall's speech and stagger, one would have thought he was drunk. He looked at his wife. Seeing her smile as they exchanged glances brought the color back to his face. His lips curved upwards on the left side of his mouth.

"Come on and lend a hand, boy," Ma said. "You might have to do this on your own in the future."

He snapped into action, shaking his head vehemently. "Ha. You and Doc are going to stay with us when the next one is due."

Her gaze darted to Doc, who smiled at her. "We'd be happy to, won't we Jenny?"

The wood burning stove in the room made it suddenly warm—at least that's what she assumed contributed to the sudden heat rising to her face. "You best be careful," Ma warned. "Any other woman would be a fool thinking you were flirting with them."

"You're not any other woman." Doc chuckled and went to showing Marshall what to do. "Which is why I have."

"Why you have what?" Ma frowned. The fool man wasn't making any sense.

"Taken a shining to you, Jenny." Doc exchanged gazes with Marshall, who looked more surprised than Ma felt. "Hoping you don't mind?" he said as he handed the baby wrapped in a blanket to Marshall. "Mind handing him to his ma?"

"Happy to." Marshall took their son to his wife. "Although, if you're thinking you want anywhere near Ma, it might be safer if you were holding her grandson. At least then she wouldn't wallop you."

"Ah, pish-posh." Ma waved her hand through the air. "I'm going to see if anything is saved from dinner. Lizzie is bound to be hungry after all the work she's done giving me my first grandchild." Ma made a clicking sound. "And if you boys are lucky, I may feed you as well."

Naomi followed her to the kitchen. Was it too much for Ma to hope that Naomi honestly wanted to help get dinner on the table? Ma suspected her daughter-in-law hoped to find out about some deep dark secret, but there was nothing to tell. Even Ma hadn't suspected that Doc had feelings for her, other than neighborly.

Ma quickly busied herself with the stew on the stove. Thankfully, someone had turned it off, but the cast iron pot was still warm. The pies on the other hand hadn't fared as well. The crumb topping she'd made and the edge of the crust was a little dark. Maybe Doc wouldn't think she was trying to impress him now, not that she wouldn't want to—if she were interested in him *that* way. She didn't have time to think about such notions.

"Can I ask you something, Ma?" Naomi carried a stack of bowls to the stove to be filled for supper.

"If it has anything to do with Doc," Ma said, her tone clipped, "I would think twice before you speak." Normally, Naomi didn't mince words, so when she didn't say anything, Ma paused filling bowls to look at her. A tear trickled down Naomi's cheek. "You weren't asking me something to meddle, were you, child?"

Naomi shook her head, causing another tear to roll down her cheek.

Sighing, Ma set the bowl down on the stove and wiped her hands on a towel before slipping an arm around Naomi and guiding her toward the kitchen table. "Let's have a seat and you can say what's on your mind."

She helped Naomi get settled on the chair at the end of the table before pulling another wooden seat around for her to sit on. Ma took Naomi's hands in hers.

Forcing a faint smile, Naomi tried to laugh. "It's really silly."

"Then tell me about it," Ma urged. She gently grasped Naomi's dainty hands. "No matter what it is, I'm here to help."

"I'm happy for Lizzie, really, I am." Naomi sniffed. "It's just... how come I can't have a baby?"

"Only the Good Lord knows." Ma squeezed Naomi's hands. "Do you remember how hard it was on Mary when they lost the baby in August?"

Naomi nodded.

"Every day she sees Sarah or Lizzie, she is reminded of her loss—just like you are. Your hands and your heart are anxious to hold your own child. Sometimes, though, God has other plans. There are other children who have lost their ma and pa and I believe in my heart that God meant for childless parents to help those children, so neither of them are lonely."

"Will Caleb think any less of me if I can't give him a son?" Deep pain wrenched Naomi, threatening to unleash more tears from her eyes.

"No." Ma shook her head. "My son will always think the world of you, and just because you aren't with child now does not mean you won't be able to have children. Maybe God knew I would need your help around here since Lizzie came to us with child, and Sarah's baby is coming soon."

"Your mother-in-law has a lot of wisdom." Doc's voice startled both of them and they jumped. "Sometimes, all a couple needs to do is stop fretting about having a baby, so they can enjoy each other's company and love, because with or without having children—you have each other."

Something about the way Doc said his piece warmed Ma's cheeks, but also gave her comfort.

CHAPTER FOUR

Doc knew Jenny was watching him as he purposely lingered, savoring each bite of her apple pie as much as he enjoyed soaking up her attention. He'd asked for a second slice because he knew she would be polite and keep him company.

"Would you like some more coffee, Doc?" Jenny glanced toward the stove. She'd already fidgeted with her hands a bit, he knew she was anxious to get up and do something—anything.

"Don't you think we've known each other long enough, Jenny, to call each other by our first names?" Doc smiled, entranced by the warmth and innocence of her greenish-brown eyes. "Please call me Thaddeus."

"Thaddeus?"

"Yes." He chuckled at the uncertainty in her voice.

"I don't think it would be wise to call you by your given name, seeing as all the townsfolk call you Doc." Jenny moved her hands to her lap, out of his reach and his sight. "I feel it would be best if I show you the same respect as the others, and I'm sorry if I've given you the wrong impression."

The bite of pie he'd taken felt like a piece of lead going down as his heart sunk with it. "I'm the one who is sorry." Doc wiped his face with the white cloth napkin and laid it on the table as he rose. "I had hoped there was the making of something like kindred spirits, if not the chance for love to blossom."

"Hmph." Jenny rose and stood behind her chair, staring at him. Her eyes were filled with emotions he couldn't quite discern. "Love and courting is something for the young folk, not old fools like us." Jenny sighed. "I had loved, once, a long time ago, but the good Lord saw fit to call him home early. But at least we had four boys to keep me busy and now I have grandchildren that will keep me busy, besides, I've got a mess of work to do to keep this ranch going."

It sounded to him like Jenny was making excuses or reasoning out why she thought she didn't need to be happy. "I've known loss as well," Doc said. "But sometimes, maybe it's good to find someone to look out after you—someone who will keep you company, so you ain't lonely."

"I'm not lonely." Ma's tone was clipped. "In fact, one would be grateful to get a moment's peace around here."

Doc nodded, a wave of sadness weighing heavy on him. "Unfortunately, I have more than enough of that at my place."

"Shame you didn't have any children when you were younger," Ma said. "They have a way of keeping you busy, even after they're grown."

"Me and the missus wanted a lot of children." It wasn't as hard to talk about as when he was younger, but it still filled him with grief. "But I lost her during childbirth, along with our daughter." Thaddeus pierced Jenny with his gaze, willing her to understand, hoping she would find it in her to move on beyond the past and her own loss. "That was the reason I decided to become a doctor—so I could help others."

"I'm sorry." Ma started to move toward him, but he turned to go and paused in his steps. Marshall was standing near the hallway leading into the room.

Their home was a little bigger than most all of the homes in the area, but with all of her family around, she didn't have a chance to be lonely. Thaddeus didn't want her pity—he wanted her affection.

"How's your young'un doing?" he asked, wanting to avoid any conversation on what Marshall may have overheard him discussing with his mother. People loved to carry on about their children, something he'd gotten used to. Just because he'd experienced loss didn't mean he couldn't be happy for others. He'd seen men drink themselves to destruction after losing a wife. Most of the ones that had other children already usually remarried again so they'd have someone to care for the children. Sometimes love developed over the years, sometimes it didn't. In his and Jenny's case, a union wouldn't have been for the children—because they were grown. Perhaps he should have pursued her years ago, when he first came here. Jenny had only been widowed a year or two back then.

"Doc?"

He startled, focusing his attention back on Marshall. "I've got a few people to check on in the area tomorrow. I'll stop by and see how your young fella is doing on my way back."

Marshall nodded. "Thanks, Doc. Me and the missus appreciate it."

"I'll make sure to make up a pot of soup." Jenny followed them to the door.

"No need," Doc said. She'd made her position clear. Jenny wasn't looking for love and she had more than enough people to occupy her time. She didn't need—or want—him. "You've got enough to take care of already and I'll only be stopping by briefly to check on your grandson."

Thaddeus grabbed his hat from a hook near the door and headed out, followed by Marshall.

"Don't mind Ma." Marshall's tone carried concern. "She just needs time to come around."

"Your Ma is a grown woman." Thaddeus stopped at his wagon and turned to face Marshall. He swallowed hard, digesting the truth. "She made her feelings clear, and while you know your ma better than I do, the one thing we both know is that she doesn't mince words. When she says something, she means it whole heartedly."

"Might be so." Marshall crossed his arms over his chest. "But she's been alone for so long, she's more apt to run from her own feelings. Pa was the only man she'd ever known, and she never expected to have feelings for anyone else. You've made your intentions known, just give it time to settle in. Once she gets used to the idea, she might stop fighting like a green broke horse. Some things take time to get used to, but she will."

CHAPTER FIVE

The next morning after breakfast, Marshall came up with a plan to talk privately with his three younger brothers. He hated lying to his brothers to get them out to the barn. Even though he did need to build a cradle for their new son, which wasn't a lie, he didn't really need all of their help. He'd used it as an excuse to get them all together to discuss something equally important. They were still waiting on Caleb. Whenever he arrived, Marshall would share his thoughts with the rest of them.

"I talked with Sarah," Jessie said. "She said you and Lizzie could use the cradle I made for our son. It'll give Jeremiah a place to sleep until we can make one for him."

Lizzie had chosen the name Jeremiah Marshall for the baby, so that he would be named after his father who passed away, and the father who was helping to raise him. Jeremiah did need a cradle. "As kind of an offer as that is, you made the cradle for your baby, and that's who should use it first." Marshall patted Jessie's back. He was happy to see Caleb stroll into the barn. "Now that we're all here, we can discuss something else. We need to talk about Ma."

Their glances all darted toward him.

"Is she all right?" Worry lines creased Montana's brow. "Did Doc say something?"

"Nothing like that." Marshall took a deep breath. "But he did express that he had feelings for Ma."

They started to whoop and holler, but Marshall settled them down. "If you're not quiet, you'll have Ma out here."

He sighed. "Thing is, Ma told him they were too old to be thinking about such notions."

"Maybe she's right." Caleb crossed his arms and leaned against one of the stalls. "She was happy with Pa. Why would she want to make a life with anyone else?"

"Because Pa's gone—he's been gone for twelve years," Marshall reminded them. "That's a long time to be alone, and Ma's worked hard to take care of us—she deserves to be happy and have someone take care of her for a change."

Two of his brothers looked contemplative. Caleb's frown deepened.

"You saw how Ma wrote to Lizzie, trying to find me a wife," Marshall said. The boys chuckled—even Caleb. Marshall might not have been happy when he'd found out what Ma did, but it all worked out in the end. Things could work out for Ma and Doc too—with a little help from them. "We don't need to do any writing—just a little nudging." Marshall smiled. "And between the four of us, we're bound to come up with something we can do to get the two of them together."

"The three of you." Caleb's lips pursed. "Count me out. I don't want a part of this."

Marshall sighed. "Suit yourself." He looked at the other two.

"Doc is coming by later today." Jessie smiled. The gleam in his eyes usually indicated he was up to something.

"You got a plan?" Marshall asked. "Or just making a statement?"

"Oh, I got a plan." Jessie chuckled. "I'm thinking we make sure the doctor stays for supper, and one of us can tell him later that we took his bag out and put it in the wagon, but don't really do it. That way he will have to come back tomorrow to get it. Gives him another reason to come by."

"And I'm sure I can develop a cough in a couple days." Montana made a terrible hacking sound that almost made Marshall wonder if he wasn't really sick.

Marshall laughed. "Good. Then it's settled. We'll all work—I mean, the three of us will work together to give the two of them a nudge. Now that we've settled that problem, I really could use some help making a cradle." He grabbed a couple boards. "Who's going to help?"

"Hold on a second." Caleb tapped Jessie with the back of his hand. "Help me get something down from the loft."

A couple minutes later they returned, carrying a cradle. Marshall blinked several times, not sure his eyes weren't deceiving him. The cradle Jessie had made for Sarah was in their room. This wasn't the same one. "What's this?"

"I made a cradle for Naomi in August, thinking I would show her I was prepared to start a family, and planned to give the cradle to her whenever she announced she was with child—but one month turned into two with no word." Pain etched Caleb's eyes. The side of his mouth twitched. "Looking at just the one cradle kept me so focused on what I didn't have, that I decided I would make one for you and Lizzie and give it to you for Christmas. It helped get my mind off of things, and it seems Lizzie was a bit anxious to get to use her present and couldn't wait."

They all chuckled, but Marshall ached for the pain in his brother's eyes. Most problems he could find a way to solve—but not that one.

CHAPTER SIX

Jenny ushered Naomi and Mary out of the kitchen to be with their husbands, or so she told them. The truth was, her mood was darker than a storm cloud. She'd spent extra effort in making fresh bread to go with the pot of soup she'd promised Thaddeus, and then he didn't show. Granted, he said he had other places to go, but she thought for sure he would come by—given he was a man of his word. Surely, he didn't let his personal feelings cloud his judgment.

He was a doctor—he made a commitment—he'd show.

The fact that he hadn't made it for dinner didn't encourage her. She remembered his words from the day before. Thaddeus told her not to bother, but she had. He was only showing concern for all she had to do—or was he hurt? Didn't he see how crazy a notion it was to think of them falling in love?

Respect. Sure. Love? Jenny almost laughed at how silly that sounded. Both she and Thaddeus were over fifty, way too old to be thinking about such things!

He said he'd been married, a fact she hadn't known about before. They both had a lot in common. Both of them had lost spouses, and they'd also lost a child, each of them a daughter. Thankfully, she still had her boys. Thaddeus on the other hand, didn't have anyone.

Even though she hadn't done anything wrong, a twinge of guilt assailed Jenny. How long had it been since she'd felt lonely—other than on nights she couldn't sleep?

Marshall's lopsided grin, or Montana's swagger would often remind her of their father. She always saw bits or pieces of him in their sons. On nights she hadn't plum exhausted herself during the day and didn't fall right to sleep—those were the nights she felt the emptiness in bed beside her. Cold nights were the loneliest, when you didn't have someone to cuddle up next to. Or, someone to really hold you so tight you couldn't move, but you didn't want to either. An ache to be held filled her.

"Are you sure you don't want any help, Ma?"

She jumped at the sound of Mary's voice and forced a smile when she turned to look at her.

"Nah, I'm fine." Jenny resisted the urge to sigh. Until yesterday, she hadn't thought of herself as anything other than Ma. Everyone called her Ma, even people who weren't her children. Perhaps that is how Doc felt in his role. Now she thought of him as Thaddeus, and he'd made her think of herself as an individual again, not just the role she filled. She loved her family and treasured them dearly. She would always be Ma to them. "How are you feeling? I noticed you didn't eat much for dinner. Are you coming down with something?" Jenny walked over and touched Mary's forehead with the back of her hand. "You don't feel warm, but perhaps we can have Doc take a look at you when he gets here."

Mary's cheeks turned rosy. She looked away and glanced back at Jenny. Her lips parted slightly.

"What is it?" Jenny asked. "It's obvious you want to tell me something."

"I… I didn't want to tell anyone until I was certain." Mary's voice quivered.

Jenny hugged her daughter-in-law. It hadn't been the kind of hug she'd been thinking of, but it was the hug she needed—along with the good news.

"When Doc comes by, we'll have him take a look at you."

Mary nodded. Happy tears trickled down her cheeks.

A smile formed on Jenny's lips and she hugged her daughter-in-law, even though she felt a sinking feeling in her gut. Why hadn't Thaddeus kept his word and come by?

CHAPTER SEVEN

The next afternoon, every time Ma thought she heard something outside, she ran to the window and looked. She'd stopped opening the door to check and see if a horse and rider or wagon rode up because the house had started to get drafty.

When Thaddeus hadn't shown up before lunch, she sent Marshall to go look for him. The old coot might think her foolish, but she didn't care. He'd made a commitment—one he hadn't kept. Since he was normally a responsible man, he'd have to expect that she'd send someone after him. Maybe she should have been the one to go look for him?

In her heart, she wanted to think he was just avoiding her, that's why he hadn't returned. But as the minutes ticked into hours and even Marshall hadn't returned by supper, her concern grew tenfold.

"I've never seen you look so troubled." Lizzie walked into the kitchen carrying Jeremiah bundled in a blanket in her arms. "Marshall will be okay."

"I know he will." Jenny nodded, mustering a reassuring smile for her daughter-in-law. She hadn't meant to scare Lizzie. The poor child was probably worried about her husband, and thought Jenny was concerned about him, too. "I'm more worried about Thaddeus."

"Thaddeus?" Lizzie squinted. "Who's that?"

"Doc." Jenny didn't like the knowing smiles that formed on her daughters-in-law's faces. She ground her teeth.

Commotion coming from the other room drew her attention. Her heart raced as she hurried to the other room.

Marshall and Montana each had one of Thaddeus' arms around the back of their neck while they held on to his waist and practically dragged him. His normally well-weathered face was pale, and he was drenched. A sinking feeling stopped her in her tracks. It took a moment to catch her breath.

She couldn't lose him—not now.

If he were dead… they wouldn't be carrying him inside.

Heaviness squeezed her chest, but she pushed past the fear threatening to drain the air from her lungs. "Put him in my room." Jenny glanced back toward her daughters-in-law. "You girls warm some of the soup broth and find all the extra blankets you can."

Hurrying after the boys, she dug into a trunk at the bottom of her bed and pulled out some of her husband's old clothes.

"Take his clothes off," Jenny said. "We need to get him out of those wet things and into some dry ones."

She started unlacing his shoes and paused when she realized the boys weren't doing as she instructed. Jenny's gaze met two pairs of piercing brown eyes.

"What?" She almost laughed. "Don't act like I ain't undressed a man before. How do you think you young'uns got here?"

"Not helping, Ma." Marshall's tone was curt. "Not helping at all."

He began unbuttoning Thaddeus' shirt.

Montana pulled him to a sitting position, so they could remove jacket and his shirt.

While they dressed him, she distracted their attention by asking questions. "What happened?"

"From what I could tell," Marshall said, "his horse must have spooked and threw him."

"He didn't have the wagon?" That seemed odd. She wondered why.

"No." Marshall shook his head. "Doc was going to head by the Parsons and it's hard to make it in a wagon unless you go the long way to get around the hills."

Marshall was right. There weren't any clear paths. The area they lived in was covered with trees and lots of hills.

"I reckon he took cover last night as best he could, but succumbed to the cold," Caleb said.

"Doc could have gotten disoriented, too." Marshall straightened after he finished buttoning the clean shirt he put on Thaddeus. "It was dark, but I don't think he hit his head. At least I couldn't find any bumps."

Ma nodded and moved closer to examine Thaddeus herself. Touching his forehead with the back of her hand revealed he was running a fever. That alone could have made him a bit delirious. When she felt around his head with both hands, she also found a small knot on the back of his head, at the base of his skull.

His eyes fluttered, trying to focus on her. "Jenny."

"Sounds like you both have gotten quite acquainted if you're calling each other by your given name." Mary's tone sounded melodic.

"You can stop getting fancy notions in your head." Jenny's words were meant for Mary but served as a reminder to herself. She'd already rejected Thaddeus. He wasn't calling out for her—he merely said the name of the person he saw when he came to—which just happened to be her.

CHAPTER EIGHT

Jenny had no idea how a person could get the chills while they were burning up with fever at the same time, but Thaddeus somehow managed. The others had already gone to bed a couple hours ago. Did she wake them?

What could they do?

Nothing.

Thaddeus had continued to slip in and out of a daze. When he did open his eyes, he was delirious, probably from the fevers. Like, now. He wrapped his arms around his chest as his teeth chattered.

"Cold," he mumbled.

"I know." Her voice was barely above a whisper. She sighed and did the only thing she knew to do—she climbed into bed next to Thaddeus and wrapped her arms around him, rubbing his arms to help him get warm.

Warmth flooded Thaddeus' body. It was a welcome relief, considering how cold he'd been out in the wilderness. Where was he now? He could hardly move, but somehow it didn't concern him.

He faded in and out of it several times before he mustered the energy to open his eyes. A flame from the lantern on the wooden table near the bed drew his attention. Someone was next to him, holding him down. He turned and saw wintery-blonde hair with streaks of silver.

Jenny.

She was asleep next to him, holding him in the comfort of her arms. No wonder he felt warm and at peace. He'd gladly freeze to death daily if it meant he would always wake up in her arms.

Thaddeus closed his eyes and drifted off to sleep.

A small gasp woke him.

His eyes opened to see a wide-eyed Naomi standing over him. Jenny was still lying next to him. This wasn't good. What could he do to save her from scandal?

"Am I dead?"

"Not yet." Naomi planted a fist on her hips. She smiled faintly. "But if any of her sons see the two of you together like this, you might be."

"Think we could keep this our little secret?"

"Sure." Her smile widened. "In exchange for a year's worth of free doctor visits."

"For the whole family?" Not that he wouldn't treat the whole family—it was a big family, and it'd give him plenty of opportunities to see Jenny.

Naomi seemed to contemplate his question. "How about for me... and the..." She glanced downward. "Well, any children that might be born in the next year... and I expect you to keep that part a secret until we're sure."

"It's a deal." Thaddeus winked at her. "Now, how about making me something to eat while I wake Jenny."

She giggled. "She got upset with us earlier when we teased her about calling you by your given name. If you ask me, it looks like you both are sweet on each other."

As Naomi left the room, his heart soared. Jenny remembered his name and used it when talking about him. She thought about him as more than just a doctor.

There was hope. '*...all things work together for good to them that love God...*' came to mind.

Maybe it took him almost dying for Jenny to realize she felt *something* for him. Gazing at her beautiful face, he carefully reached his left arm out from beneath the mound of covers and gently stroked her cheek. Her skin was soft to his touch. How he'd longed to touch her skin, feel her body close to him, for so long. It would almost be worth her sons killing him because he'd die happy. Right now, he was as close to Heaven as anyone could get.

Brown eyes fluttered open and widened when she saw him staring at her. "You're alive."

Thaddeus smiled.

"Thanks to your great care." He kissed her forehead. "But if your sons find you lying in bed next to me, I'm afraid it'll be a whole different story." A thought occurred to him. "Of course, then they might insist on a shotgun wedding." Thaddeus glanced toward the door. "Maybe I should call them?"

Jenny laughed and slapped at his arm playfully as she sat up in bed. "If you want to marry me, you old coot, just propose."

He reached for her, too woozy to sit up. His fingers gently clasped her arm before she had a chance to scoot off the bed.

She turned to meet his gaze.

"Do you mean that?" His voice was strained. His eyes searched hers. "Will you marry me?"

"I'm not about to lose you," Jenny said. Her eyes glistened. "And if I have to marry you to make sure you have somebody to take care of you—I gladly will. I can't bear the thought of losing you—or at least not admitting my feelings to you. I don't want to be alone in a house full of people."

She smiled, and a tear trickled down her cheek.

He longed to reach up and wipe it away.

"I know my family loves me, but sometimes, a woman needs another kind of love."

CHAPTER NINE

Naomi rambled on and on from the moment that Jenny told her about the proposal, then she'd gushed even more when Thaddeus came into the room, gleefully setting a plate with eggs and leftover biscuits on the table in front of him. "How about a Christmas wedding?"

"That would be a wonderful present." Thaddeus beamed.

"I already got my present," Ma said.

"What present?" Three heads turned to Caleb.

"Ma and Doc are getting married on Christmas—or maybe during Christmas Eve services." Naomi ran and hugged him. "Isn't it romantic?"

Something about the looks they exchanged concerned Jenny. "Are you all right with this?" she asked. "If you need time adjust to the news, we can put it off a bit."

She should have considered how the boys might handle the thought of having a new pa. Two weeks wasn't a lot of time—for them. For her, she'd known inside her gut she cared about Thaddeus. She didn't realize how much until she'd almost lost him.

Caleb squeezed his wife closer. "I have to admit I wasn't keen on the idea to begin with."

"To begin with?" Jenny was confused. "What are you talking about? You just found out."

Her son chuckled. "Day before yesterday, Marshall called a meeting out in the barn to see if we would all help him get you two together."

"Why that…" Jenny frowned. "Meddling in other people's business."

Thaddeus patted her hand. "That was kind of Marshall."

"It ain't like you didn't write Lizzie on his behalf, Ma." Caleb winked at her. "And it turned out fine." He shrugged. "Marshall saw a spark between you and Doc, and he wanted to give you a nudge."

"Hmph." Jenny turned her nose up. It was her place to look out for them, not the other way around. Not that it mattered now. Things were starting to work themselves out—hopefully. "If you weren't happy about it before, does that mean you've changed your mind?"

Caleb nodded. "I realized how much you cared for him and I thought about how you didn't need to spend the rest of your life alone. It was selfish of me to hold on to the past and not let you move on."

"Thank you, son." Thaddeus rose and went over to shake Caleb's hand. "I promise I'll take good care of your ma."

"I know you will." Caleb had a gleam in his eye. "Because if you don't, you'll have the Kincaid boys to deal with."

Thaddeus laughed. "I would expect no less."

"How about we wake the others and tell them the good news?" The way Naomi bubbled over with excitement, one would have thought she was the one who'd been proposed to.

Whatever the reason her daughter-in-law displayed such exuberance, Jenny took joy in seeing her happy for a change. Hopefully, she'd have some of her own good news to share soon.

Jenny had been so consumed with concern about Thaddeus, she'd forgotten that Mary had confided in her that she thought she might be with child. Hopefully Naomi could find it in her heart to be happy for her sister-in-law. Jenny sighed. That was a problem for another day. Today, they'd celebrate.

CHAPTER TEN

Christmas Eve night, Jenny sat in the pew next to her family, and her soon-to-be husband. Butterflies danced around in her stomach, moving faster than the flames flickering in all the lanterns that hung around the inside of the small, white church.

The room was never filled this much on a Sunday morning service. Either Christmas had reminded the congregation of the reason to worship and give thanks, or they'd turned out to see the wedding for themselves. She hoped they hadn't come just for the wedding—but if it was the only way to get them into church—so be it.

Even though this wasn't her first wedding, Jenny chose to wear a white dress with lace. She'd made a red bow tie for Thaddeus and told him together they would look like a candy cane—fitting for the Christmas season—and a wedding.

At the end of his sermon, Pastor Morgan announced, "There will be a wedding for those wishing to stay. I know it's getting late and most of you need to get home and get your children to bed."

Chatter floated through the room, but only one person got up to leave. It wasn't anyone Jenny knew, possibly a stranger passing through town. Other than that, it appeared everyone else intended to stay. A couple children had fallen asleep during the sermon. Jenny attributed it to the late night, not the pastor's preaching. He was always lively on Christmas sermons, when he

~ 228 ~

knew he had a congregation of people contemplating their lives and the reason for their existence.

"Are you ready?" Thaddeus squeezed her hand.

Warmth shone in his blue eyes, making her heart skip a beat. She didn't trust her ability to speak, so she nodded in response, and stood with him as he rose from the pew.

"Would either of you like to share a few words before we begin?" Pastor Morgan asked.

"Yes, Pastor." Thaddeus turned to her and took both of her hands in his. "Jenny, when I first moved to House Springs, you were one of the first people I ever talked to. You were raising four boys on your own, running a ranch, and yet you still took time out to help me get acquainted with the townsfolk. Your selflessness is one of the reasons I fell in love with you."

Sighs of adoration came from the congregation.

Jenny's heart melted.

"For all the years you've taken care of everybody else, I want to be there to take care of you, to love, honor and cherish, all the days of our lives."

A few women fanning their faces with their hands caught her attention. If Thaddeus hadn't been holding her hands, she would have had to fan her own face. "You make a woman speechless."

"And that ain't easy to do with you, Ma," someone shouted from the crowd. Laughter erupted at the response.

"Settle down." Pastor Morgan motioned with his hands. He came down off the platform and stood in front of them. "If we're ready to begin…"

They both nodded and turned to face him, Thaddeus keeping hold of her right hand. Jenny almost laughed to think he might be afraid she'd run away if he didn't hold her there. There was no way she was moving without him.

The pastor proceeded with the wedding ceremony. No sooner had he told Thaddeus that he could kiss the bride, then Sarah stood up and shouted, "The baby's coming."

Silence filled the air before it registered with everyone what she'd said.

"I now pronounce you man and wife," Pastor Morgan spoke rapidly. "Church is dismissed everyone. I reckon you may want to get your young'uns home, so they don't witness another birth on Christmas morning."

As most of the other members started to file out of the church, the Kincaids all gathered together in a huddle to address the situation at hand.

"Our family keeps getting bigger and bigger," Jenny said.

"And next year, it'll grow even more," Naomi announced. She had a hand on her currently flat stomach.

"Does that mean what I think it means?" Jenny's eyes widened.

Naomi nodded.

"That's the best Christmas present I could have asked for." Caleb lifted his wife and spun her around, kissing her as he gently set her back on the ground.

"Maybe I should wait to share my news then." Mary bit her lower lip.

"Are you?" Montana asked. When she nodded, he let out a whoop, and followed Caleb's footsteps by responding the same way, except his kiss lingered.

"You're still in church." Marshall chuckled. "You might want to save that for home."

Jenny laughed and looked at Thaddeus, who was grinning from ear to ear. "Did you know?"

"It was hard to keep a secret." He kissed her cheek and she jabbed him in the side with her elbow.

"I'm not sure I'm going to like having a doctor in the family," Jenny said. "Seems you may find out some things before I do."

"Maybe it's good for you to have a few pleasant surprises now and then." Thaddeus wiggled his eyebrows. "Just wait until you see what I got you for a wedding present." He glanced at Sarah. "It's coming special delivery."

THE END

Other Books by Susette Williams:

Mail Order Brides novelette series ~
JESSIE'S BRIDE –Book 1
MONTANA'S BRIDE –Book 2
CALEB'S BRIDE –Book 3
MARSHALL'S BRIDE–Book 4
HUSBAND OF THE BRIDE–Book 5

Texas Wildflowers novelette series ~
FREE TO LOVE –Book 1
FREE TO HEAL –Book 2
FREE TO PROTECT –Book 3
FREE TO SERVE –Book 4
FREE TO ROAM –Book 5
FREE TO FORGIVE –Book 6

The Amish Ways novelette series ~
THE WIDOWER'S NEW WIFE –Book 1
ROAD TO REDEMPTION –Book 2

Seasons of the Heart novella series ~
FALLING IN LOVE – Book 1
WINTER CHILL – Book 2
SPRING BREAK – Book 3
HEATED SUMMER – Book 4

Maid for Murder series ~
Maid for Murder: DEADLY BUSINESS – Book 1
Maid for Murder: DEADLY CONFESSIONS – Book 2

Novellas ~
ACCIDENTAL MEETING
SCROOGE FALLS IN LOVE – Typecast Christmas
series
SHADOWS OF DOUBT
MORE THAN FRIENDS
LITTLE ORPHAN ANNIE
A STITCH IN TIME

Novels ~
SOMETHING ABOUT SAM
HONORABLE INTENTIONS

Author Website: www.susettewilliams.com

Sign up for my newsletter to receive information about
new releases, contests and giveaways.

Printed in Great Britain
by Amazon

40127762R00129